The Magicians' Card

LORI ZUPPINGER

Tea & Music

This is a work of fiction. Names, characters, businesses, places, events and incidents are either the products of the author's imagination or used in a fictitious manner. Any resemblance to actual persons, living or dead, or actual events is purely coincidental.

Copyright © 2017 Lori Zuppinger
Tea & Music, Toronto
All rights reserved.

Cover art by Ann McDougall Design & Creative Services

Library and Archives Canada Cataloguing in Publication

Zuppinger, Lori, author
    The magicians' card / Lori Zuppinger.

Issued in print and electronic formats.
ISBN 978-0-9959799-0-1 (softcover).—
ISBN 978-0-9959799-1-8 (HTML)

    I. Title.

PS8649.U67M34 2017   C813'.6   C2017-903499-5
                                                                                                               C2017-903500-2

For anyone who was ever tempted to run away with the circus.

ACKNOWLEDGEMENTS

For National Novel Writing Month in November 2013, I started with a vague idea about magicians. I could not have gotten that idea from there to here without a whole lot of helpers.

To the handful of people who read this story in its first draft, especially (but not limited to) Jeannie Costello, Andria Keen and Angela Burgess: thank you for looking past the typos and dead-ends, for humouring me (often over large cups of tea) when I fixated on minor story details, and for encouraging me to release this story into the wild.

To Stephen Stanley, thank you for asking me a few years ago why I didn't write all year round the way I do in November for NaNoWriMo, for reminding me about possibilities, and most of all for the songs that are a constant source of inspiration on this creative journey.

And, of course, my husband Anthony, who has supported this crazy novel-writing thing for many years (along with all the other crazy things he didn't know he was signing up for when we met). Without his unfailing patience and encouragement, none of this would have happened. My son Duncan has also been very patient and encouraging, but he might not want to read this book till he's a little older. (He'd disapprove of the swears.)

P.S. And to Matthew Bin, who gave me the final push to jump into the world of publication when he signed my copy of *his* book with 'Waiting for you to finish *your* goddamn book so you can sign one for me!'… Thanks for the kick in the ass. Here it is.

1988

CHAPTER ONE

It was a tattered scrap of card, stuck into a crack in my Granny Chrissie's jewelry box. She had let me play with her costume jewelry many times, but I had never noticed the card before. Moving the necklaces and earrings out of the way, I pulled at it gingerly until it came free.

Whatever colours it had once had, they had all mellowed into sepia. The card was torn on the bottom, and stained, and the only word that was really legible was MAGIC. At age thirteen, it was the only word I needed.

"Granny Chrissie?" Holding the scrap reverently between my hands, I crossed the hall to the kitchen. Granny Chrissie – actually my great-grandmother, still a force to be reckoned with at eighty-six – was perched atop the small stepladder that she needed in order to reach almost anything from the upper cupboards; my height had outstripped hers somewhere before my tenth birthday.

"Oh, Heather, you'll save me the trouble. Get me down the porridge oats, lass." It was only once I had retrieved the bag of oatmeal that she noticed I was holding something. "What's that you've got there?"

With a deep breath, I held out the fragment of paper. My great-gran kept all manner of things, many of which made no sense to me – neatly folded string, washed-out milk bags awaiting reuse, Simpsons delivery boxes – but this had been in her jewelry box, not squirreled away in a closet. It must be special. "Where did this come from?"

She pushed her glasses up her nose and took it from me, clicking her tongue against her teeth when she saw what it was. "Ah, that's a long story. Do you want to hear it?"

There was something about her expression that made me think she had been waiting a long time to be asked. "Of course."

"Aye, then." She gestured to the empty pot on the stove. "You can make the breakfast, then, and the tea, and I'll tell you where that's from."

CHAPTER TWO

I spent a week every summer with Granny Chrissie – my sister did too, but never both of us at the same time, since she only had the one tiny spare room – and she had often told me little bits and pieces of her life, but this felt different. While I made the pot of porridge, she sat at the table, looking off out the window, completely silent. It was only when I sat down across from her that she appeared to remember that I was there.

"It'll be hard for you to imagine," she began at last, "but I was young once."

"I know."

She waved her hand. "No, you don't. I've been an old lady your whole life, so I know you can't picture it. But I was a girl once. That card, that's from when I was a girl, before I came to Canada. Before I met your great-granddad."

Now this was definitely something different. I couldn't remember ever hearing a story of hers that hadn't involved my great-grandfather: "my Archie", as she always referred to him. He had died when I was three, and I only barely remembered him myself, but his life had been filled in for me in rich detail. Granny Chrissie had been young when they married; it was true that it was hard to picture any life she had had before then. "How old were you?" I asked, when the pause stretched on.

"I was eighteen. It was the summer of nineteen-twenty, and I was working in Stornoway. Families like ours didn't have the luxury to go all the way through secondary school. We had to go out to work, not much older than you are now."

"What did you do?"

"I was a clerk in a shop. And lucky to get it; most of the girls back then worked gutting herring. It was too far to walk into town and home every day, so I stayed in town with my pal Ina from school; we shared a room in her auntie's house. In the attic, like. We'd have a half-day on Saturday, so when the weather was alright we'd go back to Leurbost for Saturday night and Sunday. Oh, and sometimes we'd have to get back on the Monday morning – what an hour we had to get up! About eight miles, it was. In the winter we sometimes couldn't get home for weeks at a time."

"And you didn't know Great-Granddad yet?"

She shook her head. "No. Well, yes and no. We'd met, but I didn't know him. I was supposed to marry someone else, you see."

That got my attention. "Really?"

"There was a boy from the village. Hugh MacNeil. His dad and mine were friends, and we grew up together. I'd never thought of marrying anyone else. Well, he was two year older than me, and the war was still on, then – the first war, aye? – and the moment he turned eighteen, he volunteered."

"He was killed in the war?"

Granny Chrissie shook her head. "No, that's the sad bit. He only saw a few months' duty before the armistice, and came through it, but his ship sank on the way home. It's a famous ship, the Iolaire. You could probably find it in your encyclopedia. New Year's Day, it went down."

I wasn't sure what to say about a bereavement that was nearly seventy years old, but the tiny white-haired lady across the table was starting to take on an air of drama in my mind. "That's so sad."

THE MAGICIANS' CARD

"Mmm-hm. I've not thought of Hugh MacNeil in a long time. I sometimes used to wonder how things would have gone different if he'd been on another ship, but do you know, I can't picture his face any more? People didn't have so many cameras; I never did have his photo. But back then, I thought of him every day. I was only sixteen, when he left – my dad wouldn't let me be married till I was eighteen – and I wasn't yet seventeen when he died. By eighteen I'd just about decided that I'd be a spinster till the end of my days. The other girls all went with the boys on a Saturday night – especially when the boats were in, there'd be some kind of a ceilidh on a Saturday – but I never used to go. By that summer, though, I suppose maybe I was too young to just keep on pining over my loss, and I let Ina talk me into going with her gang one night for supper, at least. Well, we were walking down to the chip shop, when we saw the queerest wagon coming through town, all painted with silver and gold and red. I'd read about gypsies in books, and that's what I thought it was: gypsies coming to Lewis, can you imagine? We all forgot about eating and a couple of the lads ran after it to try and see what it was about. They came back with a bunch of these calling cards – like the one you've got there – and said a lady was handing them out of the wagon. Of course, they were boys, seventeen and eighteen and nineteen, so all they could talk about was what she'd looked like, that she had her dress up to here and down to there," she added, gesturing to suggest a hemline that seemed quite inoffensive to me. "But I just held the card in my hand and thought it was a ticket to something out of a fairy story. Let me see it, lass."

When I passed the card back across the table, she traced her finger across it. "It's all faded away, now, and torn, but it said magicians, not just magic. 'A troupe of magicians from parts unknown – nightly performances to astound and amaze', but you can barely see where the rest of the words were, let alone read them." She flipped it over and pointed out a faint scrawl of handwriting; I had not even thought to look on the reverse. "Callanish, it says here. Do you know that painting I've got in the sitting room, of the standing stones? That's what that is. It's not so famous as Stonehenge, but it's like it. Nearly eighteen miles out of town, on the other side of the island, and that was back when there was hardly a car to be seen in the islands, and no real buses. But word was already spreading in the street, and somebody knew somebody, and by the time we'd gone back and got our supper, one of the boys had gone and fetched a friend of his who had a lorry. Well, I don't even know how many of us were piled into the thing, with all the girls in the back and the boys hanging off the running boards; it would never be allowed now, but then we couldn't drive so fast on the roads in those days. It felt like forever it took to get there."

"And the magicians were there?" I prompted, my breakfast long since forgotten.

"Aye, they were. Not right among the stones, mind – that wouldn't have been allowed even then, I think – but in the field across. There was a bunch of tents, all colours; we couldn't quite make out how they'd set it all up so fast. You had to go in to find out what was there – we couldn't see anyone outside, except for the wee booth with a lady selling tickets, but there was music coming through the air from somewhere. Most of them went to the biggest tent straight away, but I went to try and see where the music was coming from. It was like nothing I'd ever heard, even though I could only hear snatches of it until I got right up close. I finally found a tiny tent, dark blue, and looked like it was barely big enough for four or five people – I thought they must have a gramophone inside. Ina caught up with me just then, and she went in first, and I was just a second behind her, but when I got inside there were two doorways draped with silk, and no Ina. I called her name and didn't hear anything, just the music, so I went through the way that I thought the music was coming from. What a shock I had! No word of a lie, I went through the doorway and it was like I'd stepped off a cliff, except I didn't fall. I could still feel the ground I was standing on, but when I looked round it was like I was floating in space, all black and stars everywhere I looked."

She pointed at me for emphasis. "And I don't mean a painted floor or that. I mean it looked real, like open air beneath my feet. I screamed like a banshee, and then a man came through the back of the tent and said something I didn't understand, and before I knew it, the ground was back and there I was just in a wee tent with this man. I've shrunk some in my old age, but even then I was barely five feet even in my shoes, and he was probably six foot four, one of the tallest men I'd ever seen back then, and he looked like nobody I'd ever set eyes on before. He had black hair down to his shoulders and big dark eyes like Rudolph Valentino, although I didn't see Valentino in a film till I came to Canada."

"Wow."

Granny Chrissie laughed. "Aye, that's about what I thought at the time. He was so handsome he fairly took my breath away. Between that, and the shock I'd had stepping into the tent, I must have gone a bit dizzy, because the next thing I knew he was holding my arm, gentle-like, and asking if I was alright. 'Was that you doing that?', I asked him, meaning the thing on the floor. He said he was sorry I'd been so frightened, that they hadn't expected people to come from town so soon, but he didn't exactly answer my question, just talked for a while about how beautiful he thought it was on the island. I thought he was trying to calm me down, you know, since I'd had such a fright. The next thing I knew, Ina burst in – she had heard me screaming – and she looked that scandalized, seeing me in there by myself with a strange man. He said his name was Raffaele, and explained that I'd had a bit of a turn, asked her to look after me."

"And that was it?" I asked, feeling that it was a bit anticlimactic.

She shook her head. "See you, you've got no patience. Let me tell the whole story. Well, Ina dragged me out and wanted to know what had happened. I told her about the ground turning into stars, thinking she wouldn't believe me, but she did, and all she said was she'd seen something strange in the other half of the tent; she never would say what it was, but she wanted to go, she wasn't having any more of it. For all she went out to ceilidhs and went around with the boys, she was a god-fearing girl and hadn't a mite of imagination. She was set to start walking all the way back to town then and there, by herself, but I wasn't going to let her do that, as much as I wanted to stay. When we got out to the road there was a crofter who gave us a lift on his wagon most of the way. Ina didn't want to talk any more about magic or magicians, but all I could think about was how I would go back."

CHAPTER THREE

Just when I was well and truly absorbed in the story, Granny Chrissie left off, reminding me that we had a full day planned. "Aye, I'll tell you the rest, but it'll have to wait till we get back. I'm not sharing all my ancient history while we walk round the bookshop and the flea market." And as far as she was concerned, that was that. The market was usually one of my favourite parts of my summer visits, but this time I found myself only half-present; the rest of me was lost in some imagined rendition of 1920 in the Isle of Lewis. I managed to hold out until lunchtime.

"So, did you go back?" I asked, almost the moment we had sat down in the diner around the corner from the market. "To the magicians?"

Granny Chrissie gave me a wry smile as the waiter appeared. The same waiter we always had, and there was five minutes of predictable chit-chat about how tall I'd grown since last year and how school was going; eventually, we placed our orders.

Once he was safely dispatched, she nodded. "Fine; I can see this won't wait till we get home. Yes, I went back. I wasn't sure how I'd manage it, but Lewis was a small place – still is. Word travelled fast, and soon most everyone was talking of nothing but the carnival out at Callanish. I had thought I would have to wait till the next Saturday, with my half-day, but by the Tuesday, there was word that the magicians were sending their wagon to and from town, to take people there, for a couple of pence. Well, I ran back to my rooms at my dinner break and told Ina's auntie that I wouldn't be in for supper, and the moment we shut up the shop for the day, I was away. Most of them taking the wagon were young folks, like me."

"I guess there wasn't usually much going on that was that exciting," I said, twisting my straw.

"True, but not just that," she replied. "We'd just been through a war, and all but the youngest lads had seen it. There was no one who hadn't lost family, friends. And lots of young folk scraping for work, having to leave the islands. We all needed an escape. Well, we got to Callanish and there were all the tents again, but I could have sworn they'd been rearranged. I put my coins in the box and went looking around. Everything was amazing – I couldn't even explain to you all the things I saw – but I was really looking for that one wee tent I'd been in before. It didn't seem to be where I'd seen it before, but there were so many people and so much noise now, it fair did my head in."

"Did you find him?"

"Eventually. Just when I was about to give it up, I heard that same music again, and there was that blue tent. I stepped in expecting the trick with the floor, but this time it was like a corner of a garden; I could even smell the flowers. And Raffaele was sitting there on a bench. 'I wondered when you would be back, Chrissie Morrison,' he said to me, even though I was sure I'd never told him my name." There was an interruption, then, as the waiter came back with our food.

"And then what?" I prompted, as soon as the coast was clear.

"He took me round the show, showed me the things I hadn't seen – little details I hadn't noticed. And then we went out walking away from the crowd, to the stones. Raffaele asked me so many questions – about myself, my family, about living in the islands, how to say things in the Gaelic – so many that it seemed I'd never get a chance to find out anything about him. I couldn't make out why my life would be so interesting, to someone like that. He wanted to know what I knew about the standing stones, but that I couldn't tell much. I'd only really been there once before the magicians came. Well, he said I should see them properly, and took me by the hand and led me right up to them, had me lay my hand on the stones. I could see some other folk doing it – some of the magicians, I thought. I saw the lady who'd taken our tickets. Everything about the night just seemed that strange. Even the moon, when it would come out from behind the clouds. The next day, I might have thought I'd dreamt it all, if it weren't for the whole of the town being all a-twitter about the carnival at Callanish."

Granny Chrissie was looking off into the middle distance, as if she was lost in memory. "You don't need all the details, but I went back to the magicians every night for the week, and the next. Most of the young ones did; I even caught Ina there once or twice more, though she said she was just trying to find me. But then Ina's auntie found out where I'd been going, and her auntie wrote to my mum, and my father was half ready to drag me back to Leurbost, if it hadn't been for my job. My parents were old-fashioned even for those days – they were already near forty by the time I came along – and they didn't even like me living in town on my own, much less running about with a bunch of strange folk doing magic. And I fell out with Ina, since I blamed her for blabbing to her auntie; it got bad enough that I had to find a room somewhere else. But I didn't care about any of it. I'd been swept off my feet. And then…"

"And then…?"

She sighed. "One night came, and we found them packing their things. It was time to move on, Raffaele said. I half hoped that he'd ask me to run away with him. He kissed me, and said sweet things, but then it was goodbye. I was young, and naïve, and thought he loved me like I thought I was in love with him. I didn't realize back then that there's a lot of men who've a girl in every port, as they say. Sometimes more than one."

"What do you mean?"

"Oh, I heard some whispers later that there'd been others romanced by him while the magicians were on the island, even as short a time as it was. It was an education."

"Oh." Even though I knew that obviously she had not run away with Raffaele the magician, the ending seemed to fall flat. "And you never heard from him again?"

Granny Chrissie shook her head. "I never did. No one did, nor any word of any of the magicians. It was as if they came out of the clear blue sky one day and then just disappeared the very same way. We all went back to our workaday lives, though we talked about it often at first. For most folk, it was like a splendid party; everyone remembered it fondly but seemed kind of glad to be back to normal. But I felt like it had just shone a light on everything that was dull about my life."

"That's so depressing."

"Do you think so, lass? I look back and think it was the kick in the pants I needed. I don't know that I really wanted to run away with the circus – though I thought I did, at the time – but I didn't want to spend my life a spinster clerk in a dressmaker's, renting a garret room, never going more than thirty miles from Stornoway, either. I heard that Ina was away to Glasgow all of a sudden, and that was the last straw – we had never spoken again, you see, and I was cross enough at her that it stuck in my throat that she was off to the city and I wasn't. That autumn I met Archie MacDonald again, and gave him a second look. I let him walk me home now and then, and found that a boy didn't have to be dark and mysterious to know how to treat a girl. And he had ambition; he was already talking then about getting off the island and settling somewhere like Australia or Canada. By the spring, we were married, and two years later we sailed on the Metagama with three hundred others, Canada-bound. My Archie was a good man, and we did well for ourselves here, had our family, and made a good life. I think of all the places we travelled together, once the children were grown, and of some of my school chums who barely went further than Edinburgh in their lives. No, I've no complaints, none at all. The magicians gave me something to dream on, and a time in my life I'll never forget, and that's why I still have that bit of card tucked away. But I've no regrets. That's maybe hard to understand at your age, but when you're grown, it'll make more sense."

I thought it over. "I guess if you'd gone away with Raffaele, I never would have existed."

She reached her wizened little hand across the table and patted my arm. "That's true, lass, and I'm glad you do."

1996

CHAPTER FOUR

I ignored the phone when it rang. After procrastinating for the better part of the day, I was finally making some progress on my biology readings and wanted to get through them in time to go to Sneaky Dee's for Wednesday night bingo. But it was not to be. My roommate was calling my name up the stairs.

"Got it," I yelled back, as I picked up the receiver. "Hello?"

It was my dad's voice on the other end. "Hi, honey."

"What's up?" Usually it was my mum who called: only once a week or so, now that I was in second year and they were getting accustomed to me being away at school. If Dad was calling, something must be wrong.

"It's Granny Chrissie, honey. She's in the hospital again, and they're saying..." His voice faltered, ever so slightly. "It looks like this is the end. I know you're in the middle of the term and it's not easy for you to get away, but if you want to say goodbye..."

I swallowed. She was ninety-four now, and had been in failing health since my last year of high school, so the call shouldn't have come as a shock – but still, there was a sense of unreality to it. "How long does she have?"

"It's hard to say, but the doctor thinks it might only be a day or two. I can drive in and pick you up and bring you back tonight if you want to come; I thought you might miss less time that way than taking the bus down. You don't have classes tonight, do you?"

Somehow that brought me to attention; if Dad was willing to drive into Toronto, in the snow, in the tail end of rush hour to get me, it must be serious. "No – I mean, no, I don't have class tonight. I'd like to come."

I attempted to continue my homework while I waited for my father to arrive, but my attention was no longer on it. At twenty-one I was old enough to understand mortality, and I'd had other relatives pass away, but somehow part of me had thought that my great-grandmother would keep soldiering on forever. Even as her health and mobility and eyesight had diminished, her brain had stayed as sharp as ever. I tried to articulate this to my dad on the drive back to Kitchener.

"I know what you mean, Heather," he said, not taking his eyes off the falling snow and the westbound traffic. "She's a tough old bird, but… I saw her today, just before I called you, and I think she's ready. All her contemporaries are long gone, and she's already seen one of her children go before her. She was more concerned about what dress we'd put her in for the funeral. 'I don't want to be wearing that old pink thing when I see my Archie again! Make sure they put me in the green!'," he recounted, with a fair imitation of her accent and tone. "I think she reminded everyone, including the nurses."

"That sounds like her." I laughed, but not really. She had told me many times that she'd given up 'the kirk', so I didn't know whether she still expected to go to heaven or some other kind of afterlife – I certainly wasn't sure what I thought about it all – but I did hope that she'd somehow see my great-granddad again.

Going into the hospital was unsettling. It had the atmosphere of a sombre sort of party, there were so many people there: aunts and uncles and cousins coming in and out of Granny Chrissie's room, congregated in the waiting area, and asking questions at the nurse's station. "The nurses must be getting sick of all of us," I said quietly, not really wanting to face a full family reunion in that particular setting. Thankfully my dad managed to slip me by most of the crowd and into the dimness of the hospital room.

My Gran was there at the bedside with my Grandpa Marcel – not technically my grandfather, but my dad's father had died young and my grandmother had remarried – and Marcel patted Granny Chrissie's good arm, the one that didn't have a tube going into it. "Heather's here, Chrissie. You wanted to see her."

"Oh, good. Give us a minute alone, the lot of you, before the visiting hours are done." Once they had left, she took a rasping breath. "Sit down here, lass. I can't see but shadows any more, but I can hear you fine. I hope you're not missing too much of your schoolwork to come and see me."

Her voice was weak, but she was as sharp and practical as ever; it put me a little more at ease. "Not too much. Dad's going to take me back to Toronto tonight so I don't miss my morning classes."

"Aye, that's good. I'm proud of you, Heather. You know your dad was the first in our family to go to university, and I'm glad you're following him. I've had more out of this life than I'd any right to ask for, but that's the thing I would have liked to do, if I'd been born in the right time and place, is get my education. But I've had a good run. Have they told you that I'm dying?" She said it in the same tone as I might use to ask someone if they knew that I was from Kitchener.

"Yes."

"Well, I am, and that's alright," she replied. "You're only young and I know that won't make sense to you, but I've been on borrowed time for years now. All I want now is to say my goodbyes, and you can see they've all come. There's only one other thing, that I need you for, particularly."

"What is it?"

"Do you remember when I told you the story about the magicians?"

I nodded at first, forgetting she could barely see. "Yes."

"Well, do you know I've never told anyone else that story, in all these years? All the other people who saw them – your great-granddad, my school pals, everyone I knew in Stornoway – they're all long gone, and none of them ever heard all that I saw there. And now that I'm at the end, I'd hate to think that was going to go out of the world. So I want you to promise to remember it for me."

"I will."

"I mean it, lass." There was urgency in her voice now. "Do you know why I told you the story?"

"Because I found the card. I asked you about it."

She shook her head. "You weren't the only child to go playing with my jewelry and come across it. I nearly told you the same thing as the others – that it was just an old magic show – but you know, I looked at you and thought you were maybe the only one who would understand. I didn't want them to think I'd taken leave of my senses," she added, with what was probably meant to be a laugh but came out as a cough. "I only wish you could have seen it. That's the one thing I've wondered, all these years - where did they go?"

There was a sound of footsteps at the door, and I knew I should give the rest of the family a chance to come in. "I'll remember, Granny Chrissie, I promise."

CHAPTER FIVE

Granny Chrissie died that night, while my dad and I were probably halfway back to Toronto. My mum said that she had held on just long enough to see everyone who was able to come, and then passed peacefully, with a smile on her face. I supposed that it was the best way to go; ninety-four was certainly a long life, and hers had been a full one.

A week later, I returned to Kitchener for the memorial. It was as upbeat an affair as possible, with food and stories and a slideshow of Granny Chrissie throughout her lifetime. There were many photos I had never seen before, but one in particular struck me: a yellowed, scratched black-and-white of a young couple, with a ship in the background. "That's the ship that brought them to Canada," my gran said, coming to sit down beside me. "She was already expecting Hector then, though they didn't know it yet. Mum had never been off the island before, so the whole way across the Atlantic she thought she was just seasick. He was born in November, and then me the next October. They called us Irish twins."

"So that was taken in Stornoway?" I asked, as the image switched on to a more recent one.

Gran nodded. "As far as I know, that's the only picture of her in Scotland. Well, when she lived there, that is – obviously there's photos from when she went back to visit, but that was years and years later. She said there were all sorts of photographers there that day; it was a big news event since so many young people were emigrating."

"Is there any way… could I get a copy of that picture?" I asked.

She looked pleased. "Of course. Nancy was going to get prints made of some of the slides for your dad and everybody; we didn't know if any of the kids would want them, but I'll tell her to get another set for you."

I was still watching the slide show, wondering how many different images there were to go through before it would cycle back to the Stornoway dockside, and didn't notice my gran pulling something out of her purse until she put it in my hands. It was an envelope with my name on it, the handwriting perfect and old-fashioned. Granny Chrissie's writing, but not done too recently: Christmas and birthday cards from her the last three or four years had been witness to the increasing tremor in her hands. "What is this?"

"I don't know. When she moved into the home and we were cleaning out her things from the house, I found this in her jewelry box, sealed with your name on it. I asked Mum about it at the time and all she said was that I was to keep it in a safe place and give it to you… well, when her time came." She took a moment to dab at her eyes with a tissue, although her voice wavered only slightly. "She said you'd know what it was."

Though I could sense her curiosity, this wasn't the place to open the envelope. The only thing Granny Chrissie could possibly have sealed away for me specifically would be the tattered remains of the magicians' card, now that I knew that I was the only living person who knew the whole story. I wasn't sure she had intended me to keep it a secret forever, but if she hadn't confided in her only daughter, I didn't think it was my place to invite questions right away. "I'll open it at home," I replied, tucking it carefully into my messenger bag.

Two weeks later, a second envelope arrived; this one was stiff manila with a large DO NOT BEND notice, and a return address from my Aunt Nancy. Inside were perhaps two dozen photos, blown up to five by seven size. I shuffled quickly through until I came to the one I wanted to see again. On the back, in my aunt's tidy schoolteacher hand, it said 'Archie and Chrissie MacDonald, boarding the S.S. Metagama, Stornoway Pier, Isle of Lewis, Scotland, April 21, 1923'.

They both looked like strangers to me, at least at first. When I took the photo to my desk, in the better light, and studied it a while, I could recognize my great-grandmother's features. She had been tiny even then; I knew my great-grandfather hadn't been a particularly tall man, but he towered over her. Her face was half-turned towards him, and their arms were linked together, both of them smiling – equal parts excitement and apprehension, I imagined. They were the same age, which meant that Archie hadn't been old enough to have served in the war; it was the first trip off the island for both of them, and they were going half a world away. It struck me suddenly that they were the same age in the photo that I was at that moment. I had seen more of the world, but Chrissie – I couldn't think of her as 'Granny' and a young woman at the same time – was not only married, pregnant, and about to move to a foreign country, but she also had a drowned fiancé and a brief romance with a mysterious magician to her credit. I still felt like barely more than a kid.

I put the photo and the magicians' card together in a frame, and mounted it on the wall above my desk. The story was unforgettable in any case, but I liked looking at the image. I wished that she had shown it to me herself; there were so many more questions I wanted to ask.

My dad called several weeks later to say that Granny Chrissie's will had been settled. "She had more investments than we'd realized, and they'd made some smart decisions years ago," he told me. "I won't bore you with all the details, but she's left you – and each of the great-grandchildren – seventy thousand dollars."

"Seventy? Seven-zero?" I asked, trying not to choke on the gum I'd been chewing.

"Yes, seven-zero. Frankly, I was a little surprised myself," he replied. "If you handle it wisely, this could go a long way towards buying yourself a house when you're done your studies, even if you stay in Toronto."

I had just barely begun to envision a future without student loans. "Wow. Yeah. I mean, I guess so, that's a good idea."

"Listen, honey, I know it's a lot to take in. And you're an adult, you can make your own decisions about what to do with the money, but if you want any guidance…"

"Yes, please. But I think…" I paused, then started again. "I think I'll take a little of it and go travelling this summer."

"That's a good idea. Backpacking round Europe?"

"I want to go to Scotland." It was odd that I'd never been. My parents had taken my sister and me to Florida, the Caribbean, all over Canada, and even to France, but never Scotland despite all my dad's family having come from there. And the more I looked at that old photo of my young great-grandmother, the more I wanted to go to Lewis, specifically, and see where she had lived.

CHAPTER SIX

As soon as my exam schedule came out, I booked a plane ticket, and as the term wound down the travel planning began to consume all of the time that wasn't already taken up with studying and coursework. I was reading every guidebook I could find, running up my phone bill calling overseas to book hostels, and even using the library computer lab to find a little bit of information on the World Wide Web, but bit by bit the itinerary came together: some time to travel around and see the sights, and some time to connect with my roots.

Thinking on our family background made me realize that my trip could cover more than one base; we had another Scottish connection, one that I knew less about. The next time my mum called me, I asked to speak to my dad as well. "Dad, I was wondering something about your dad. Your real dad, I mean, not Grandpa Marcel." Marcel had come into their lives when my father was still young; he called Marcel 'dad', and it hadn't been until I was twelve or so that I'd found out he was my dad's stepfather. "Do you know where in Scotland he came from? Or should I ask Gran?"

My dad exhaled heavily. "Probably best not to ask her about him. I was too young to really understand much of it at the time, but… well, let's say my parents didn't have a happy marriage. As hard as it was for my mum to be a widow with three young kids, I think she was better off without him, as terrible as that sounds."

"Wow, I had no idea."

"Don Ross – my father - was the type Granny Chrissie would've called a 'hard man'. Intellectually, with what I learned about him later, after I'd grown up, I suppose I can understand some of it. He was born out of wedlock, for starters – I looked up his birth certificate once, since Mum would never talk about him – and I don't think I need to tell you how that would've been looked at in nineteen-twenty-one. Then he grew up in the Depression, went into the service in World War Two and got discharged for reasons I don't know. By the time he came over here after the war, he'd had a rough life. They say I look like him: the dark hair, at least, and the height; it's probably his genes that you have to thank for being so much taller than your mum, or your gran. But you wanted to know where he was from, sorry. He was born in Glasgow, on Crown Street – and I think he stayed there with his mother till he went into the army. I don't know anything about his mother other than her name, Murdina Ross."

"Murdina? That's an unfortunate name." I was scratching it down on a scrap of paper, along with the other details. "Thanks, Dad. I'll see if I can find Crown Street when I get to Glasgow."

Finally, the day after my final exam, it was time to get on a plane. Things seemed to be falling into place when I boarded the flight and found myself sitting next to an elderly lady named Margaret who told me that she was originally from Harris – which was rather confusingly considered a different island from Lewis even though they shared the same landmass. "My great-grandmother was from Lewis," I told her, after the flight safety demonstration. "It's my first time going to Scotland. Oh, and my grandfather was from Glasgow," I added, as an afterthought, "but I never knew him."

"Are you going to Lewis, yourself?"

"I'm doing a bit of sightseeing first, but yes. My great-granny told me some stories from when she was a girl there… I'd like to see it for myself."

"Good for you, hen," Margaret replied. "It's a bit off the beaten track; not too many visitors venture out that far. Whereabouts did she stay?"

"She was from Leurbost, but then she moved to Stornoway when she started working. They came to Canada in nineteen-twenty-three, though."

"Oh, Leurbost," she said, pronouncing it slightly differently. "I was born in Rhenigidale – what an isolated spot! Beautiful place, but I had to move away to find work. I've been in Ayrshire since I was first married. My sons are both in Canada now, though. Did you say it was 'twenty-three, that your great-grandmother came over? She must have been on the Metagama, was she?" When I nodded – a little surprised – she went on. "That was a famous ship. I was just a wee girl at the time, but people talked of it for years. Oh, and she would have been still on Lewis when the magicians came. Did she ever talk of it?"

Now I was quite astonished. "Yes, she did. No one else in the family knew about it, though. I happened to find their card tucked away in her jewelry box when I was thirteen, and she told me the story. She… she just passed away a few months ago, and she left the card to me. Did you know anyone who saw them?"

Margaret smiled. "Well, it was a strange thing. Everyone seemed to know about it and talk of it, but no one quite admitted to having gone. I was only just born when they came, so it was years past by the time I heard tell of it, but by then it had sort of a whiff of scandal. The islands were straight-laced then – still are, compared to a lot of places – and the kirk frowned on that sort of thing. It was mostly the young, unmarried folks who went to see the show, of course, and there were rumours that things were going on that young, unmarried folks weren't supposed to be getting up to. As if that never happened anywhere else," she added, with a chuckle. "I used to wish that I'd been born early enough to go. By the time they came back, I wished I'd been young enough to go."

"They came back?" No one had ever said anything about them coming back. "My Granny Chrissie said that they were never heard from again."

"I suppose she would have been in Canada then. I was in Largs. It was... oh, let me see, when was it now? 'Fifty-seven, 'fifty-eight, maybe. I had my two boys still in school and a baby on the way. It was just a thing I heard about after the fact anyway, just a second-hand mention in a letter from an old friend who'd moved away as well, but even if I had known it's not like I could have gone running off to the isles to satisfy my curiosity. Oh dear," she added, trying to cover up a huge yawn. "You'll have to excuse me; I always take a wee sleeping pill just before I go on a long flight."

She didn't seem to think of what she had just told me as anything more than the merest of curiosities, but I needed some time to digest this revelation. If they had come back – if that was indeed what had happened – in the 1950s, might they have come back at other times? I wondered if any photos existed. If the Raffaele who Granny Chrissie had met had been a young man in 1920, he might have still been with them when they returned; I would have loved to put a face to the name.

I eventually fell asleep somewhere over the Atlantic, my head full of strange images.

CHAPTER SEVEN

The rush of excitement at being in a different country on my own managed to put the thoughts of the magicians temporarily on the back burner once I arrived. Glasgow was my first stop, and at the tourist information centre I asked about the location of Crown Street. "My grandfather was born there," I added, when the clerk behind the desk pulled out a map and frowned slightly.

"Aye? There's not much to see there, if you were thinking to look up his old address," the young man replied. "They knocked down most of the old Gorbals tenements and built tower blocks years ago; now they're taking some of those down as well. You'd be better off going to the People's Palace; it's a museum where you can see what life was like." I took his suggestion, but although the exhibits were interesting, it wasn't quite the dramatic personal connection I was looking for.

However, between Glasgow, Edinburgh, and a backpackers' bus tour through the Highlands, I had no trouble falling in love with Scotland. After two weeks of touring round, though, the time came to finally get to the real point of my trip. I took a train north to Inverness and a bus from there to a little town called Ullapool, from which I would catch a ferry to Stornoway. I knew from the printed timetables and from the maps that it was a relatively long distance – the boat would take nearly three hours – but still I was surprised to see the size of the vessel pulling up to the pier as I stepped down from the bus. It was more like a cruise ship to my eyes, and the transport trucks lined up to drive aboard were dwarfed against it. I began to get a better sense of just how remote the Outer Hebrides were.

Planning the trip, I had had visions of some kind of romantic homecoming, catching a first glimpse of Stornoway in the late afternoon sunshine from the bow of a boat, perhaps with some music playing in the distance. In reality, it had been a steady drizzle from the moment I boarded the bus in Inverness, and for most of the ferry ride my only view was fog from the windows of the cafeteria. When we pulled into the harbour, I saw fishing boats docked in front of a tidy-looking town, not particularly different from other small towns I'd seen on my travels so far. The rain was still coming on steadily, now blown half-horizontal by a chilly west wind, and it was after eight in the evening. Discoveries could wait; for now, I just focused on finding my way to the youth hostel, dry clothes and a warm bed.

The next day was Sunday, and as I'd been forewarned, Stornoway was something of a ghost town, with the only signs of life being in the vicinity of the churches. However, the rain had cleared away and the sun was peeking through here and there, showing the town in a far more promising light. The tourist information office was closed, like everything else, but there was a small rack outside where I at least found a map to help me get my bearings. I found Point Street, where Granny Chrissie had rented a room from her friend's aunt; I wished I had thought to ask the exact address, but still, I could imagine her staying in one of these buildings, walking to work, maybe dreaming of adventure. I had no idea what shop she had worked in or where it had been, but it was a small town even still. At the harbour, near where I had gotten off the ferry the evening before, everything looked more like a postcard view when the sun hit it. I took a few photos, knowing they probably wouldn't do it justice when I got them developed.

Lunchtime posed a problem, with the town shuttered up for the day, but a group of teenagers eating takeout food pointed to at least some exceptions. After a bit of wandering around, I was surprised to find a small takeaway counter that was open. A line-up stretched out into the narrow pedestrian alley; while I was waiting, I peered at the thicket of posters and flyers stuck to a noticeboard just inside the window, till something caught my eye.

I had to wait until my position in the queue brought me inside the shop and within arm's reach of the board to see what it was, but there was just a corner of something sticking out, with an old-fashioned font that looked familiar. When I came close, I gently lifted the corner of an ad for child minding to see what was layered underneath.

It hadn't been my imagination: it said MAGICIANS, in just the same lettering as on the fragment of card that Granny Chrissie had left me. But this wasn't so old. It was a clean, cream-coloured card that was unquestionably modern. Tempting though it was to tear it down and examine it more closely, I had to move along with the line. After giving my order, I decided to ask the girl behind the counter. "Has there been a group of magicians here, recently? I saw the flyer on the board there."

"Last autumn," she replied, brightening up visibly. "They were brilliant. They were here for about a fortnight. Most exciting thing that's happened here in ages. I wish they'd come back." She handed me my rice and curry, and took my money: time for the chit-chat to end.

"Thanks," I replied, still tempted to go back and tear the card from the board.

CHAPTER EIGHT

I woke up the next day with one thought in mind – the magicians had been there just months before. For eight years, I had thought I knew as much of the story as there was to know, that it had been a mysterious one-off occurrence in 1920. But they had been back twice – or at least twice. For all I knew there might have been other times. This changed everything.

The twenties were virtually out of living memory, and the fifties were distant, but 1995 – if they had been on Lewis in the past year, then surely there must be some record of it. There must be something. I did what any good student would do, and found the nearest library. And then discovered that it was closed on Mondays. Was nothing ever open here? Fortunately, the rest of the town was business as usual.

"This is kind of a strange question," I announced to the young man at the desk of the tourist information office. "But I'm wondering about an event that happened last year – in the fall, I think? A group of magicians… I wondered if you had any information about them."

He blinked at me, and took a second to answer. "Well… yes and no. I remember them being here, and there were posters about, but they never provided us with any information; it wasn't on any of the official guides or any of our listings that we get internally. It was the strangest thing, because usually if there's anything going on that visitors might want to see, they're after us to promote it."

Somehow I wasn't surprised. "Do you recall when, exactly, they were here? I'm... uh... doing some research on them. I thought I might go by the library tomorrow and see if I can find out anything."

Pursing his lips, he pondered. "October. Around the middle of October. I didn't see them myself; I was working and doing uni courses, and thought I would go and see them when I got the time, but they were gone as quick as they appeared, and I missed my chance. Sorry," he added. "Do you need directions to the library?"

"No thanks; I've got it."

Since the library was going to have to wait till the morrow, I decided to go and see the village where my great-grandmother was born. Leurbost was about a twenty-minute bus ride from town, a little handful of homes strung out like a necklace along a narrow back road, parallel to a long inlet from the sea. The houses were plain and solid and relatively modern-looking; it was hard to guess whether any of them would have been standing at the time Granny Chrissie had been a girl. There was half an hour to wait before the bus would be back, so I wandered down the road a little further, snapping photos as I went. This place was close to Stornoway now, a short bus ride or even less by car, but once it had been far enough that Granny Chrissie had had to move into town – too far to come home, except occasionally on the weekend. It was hard to picture a world so small.

Looking through the camera viewfinder, I didn't realize anyone was approaching until the bicycle pulled up beside me. "We don't often get visitors here. Sorry, didn't mean to startle you."

I turned to see a middle-aged woman wearing a bike helmet and a thick wool sweater. "My family came from here, a long time ago," I explained. "I don't know what house or anything, though, or even if the house is still around."

"What's your name?"

"Heather Ross," I replied. "But it wasn't the Ross side; my great-grandmother was Chrissie Morrison, then Chrissie MacDonald after she got married. She was born in nineteen-oh-two."

"Morrison? Well, then, we must be distant relations. I was a Morrison before I was married, too. I'm Sarah Smith, now. The old house is gone, but it was down near that bend in the road. We used to play around the last of the foundation when we were kids."

"I guess it's somebody's backyard now."

She laughed. "It's my dad's backyard. Go on and have a look if you like; he won't be bothered, so long as you shut the gate behind you."

I felt a bit nervous of venturing onto somebody's land, but Sarah cycled on ahead of me to the house and gestured for me to go ahead, before she headed inside. So, with some sense of awkwardness, I opened the gate – making sure to close it – and went looking for the remains of the old house. It wasn't really a backyard as I thought of the term, more of a scrubby field; a few sheep were visible here and there, and a contour of irregular grass suggested a place to look.

It was a tumbled-down outline of stones, but I could still make out the general layout of it; a long narrow rectangle, divided near the middle. I stood inside, trying to pretend that I was looking out a window at the fields and the water. Granny Chrissie had come a long way from here.

I half-hoped that Sarah or her father would come out; I was already kicking myself for not asking if she had seen the magicians. They were watching out the big front window as I came back out of the driveway, so I gave a wave before walking back up to the bus stop. It was a start.

First thing the next morning, though, I was at the Stornoway library, practically the moment they opened their doors. I asked the librarian at the desk for local newspapers and was shown to a microfilm machine with reels of the Stornoway Gazette. It was a weekly paper, so it didn't take too long to narrow things down to the issues of the previous October. Nothing in the first week. Nothing in the second. But in the third week of the month, I found it:

MAGICIANS 'ASTOUND AND AMAZE'

Last week, a group of travelling magicians arrived on Lewis and set up on the property of Angus Murray of Calanais, after having been denied permission to mount their show nearer to the standing stones. Although Mr. Murray was surprised at the request, he says that as it is late in the season, his fields are "not needed, so may as well be put to use". Put to use they have been indeed, as magic shows are being mounted nightly, apart from Sundays, and attracting audiences from all over Lewis and Harris and even further afield. Stornoway students Emma MacLeod and Kirsty Smith, both sixteen and attending the Nicolson Institute, have attended the performances each night and describe it as "unbelievable, like something out of a film". The performers declined to be interviewed or to say how long the show will run. Tickets are £6 at the door.

Six pounds seemed a bargain. If only they had come a few months later! I continued searching, in case there might be more information, or a picture, but to no avail. I didn't think that looking up a pair of high school students would be socially acceptable, curious though I was about what they had seen there; attending the show every night, they reminded me of Granny Chrissie's tale.

Instead, I asked the librarian. She volunteered that she had attended the show once, and offered her opinion that it had to have been done with 'some kind of special effects', since it could not have possibly been real.

"Did you happen to take any photos?"

She shook her head. "It was too dark. I knew a few people who tried to get snapshots, but none that turned out. I wish someone could have caught how they did it all, though."

Almost as an afterthought, I remembered my conversation with Margaret on the airplane. What date had she said? 1957 or '58. That was a little more ground to cover than a specific month of last year, but I had some time; I asked the librarian if they had reels from the 1950s.

It took a bit of wading through, but the papers were interesting in their own right; every few minutes I would get distracted by the period advertisements. In the end, I nearly missed it since it didn't have 'magician' in the title.

SENSATION AT CALLANISH

Beginning Tuesday last and concluding on Friday, a magic show was mounted at Callanish and enjoyed by young and old alike. Spectators reported on the novelty of the illusions on show.

Just a brief mention, but it established a date in April of 1957. I noted this down in my travel journal and, emboldened by my modest success, asked the librarian for the issues from 1920.

AN UNUSUAL ENTERTAINMENT

A troupe of carnival performers arrived at Stornoway on the S.S. Sheila on Saturday, 26 June and proceeded to Callanish where they erected a field of tents close by the stone circle. Since that time, they have been giving entertainments each evening saving Sunday. Included in their demonstrations are several magic-tricks and novel musical performances. Visitors have come from as far as Obbe to see the remarkable show.

It was tantalizing to find these, but they left me only slightly better informed than I had been before.

The next day I went on the final leg of my pilgrimage, taking the bus to the Callanish Stones. Every guidebook had described them as a must-see in this part of the world, and they certainly did not disappoint. Sitting on a slight rise of land, the stones towered over me, a ring with a long avenue extending from it. It was easy to imagine the place having its own magic – even though I did arrive at roughly the same time as a busload of elderly tourists. To escape the brief rush of people, I followed a printed map from the visitor centre to a smaller, satellite grouping of stones in a field a few hundred metres away. The stones here were impressive as well, but less overwhelming, leaving me at leisure to ponder the view.

One of my books had described Lewis as a 'drowned landscape', and I could see their point: everywhere I looked there were sea inlets and small lakes and ponds, with plenty of what looked like low, boggy terrain in between. The higher ground – none of which was what I would call particularly high – was a mix of tough, scrubby grass, heather, and the large yellow-flowering gorse bushes that boasted impressive spikes at a closer glance. The colours of the land were subtle and muted, in partnership with the high grey overcast of the sky. It was the sort of place that I could imagine someone finding either fiercely beautiful, or intensely depressing; I made a choice to see the former.

There was something about this place that had drawn the magicians back three times – or at least three times, that I knew of. I wasn't sure exactly what it was, but I thought I felt it too. Leaning against the rough surface of one of the upright stones, I gave a little vote of thanks to Granny Chrissie, wherever she was now, for bringing me here.

2001

CHAPTER NINE

After my trip to Scotland, the idea of the magicians fell into place in the background of my life as I did all the things the world told me I was supposed to do: finished my degree, joined the working world, and bought a tiny fixer-upper house with the help of Granny Chrissie's money and my dad's cosign on the mortgage. It was only when I invited a new boyfriend over for dinner one night that the lid was opened on the story once more.

"Are these your grandparents?"

"That's nineteen-twenty-three, Alan; how old do you think I am?" I laughed, and handed him a glass of wine. "They're my great-grandparents, leaving Scotland to come to Canada."

He picked up the picture frame off the bookshelf. "What's this card, in with the photo?"

I had only just moved the picture to a more visible spot, and it was the first time anyone had asked about it. "It was… a keepsake she left me. A group of magicians that came to the Isle of Lewis when she was eighteen. She kept that till she died."

Alan raised an eyebrow and set the picture back in place. "Hm. Must have been some kind of magic show."

The offhand conversation stayed in my head all evening. When Alan had gone home, I sat down at my computer desk, opened a browser window and typed in *Isle of Lewis magicians* on a whim.

Perhaps not surprisingly, the results offered me a full page of magicians for hire for children's birthday parties. So did the second page, and the third. I decided to try again.

Magicians Callanish gave me excerpts from fantasy books.

Magicians Lewis 1920: nothing that was remotely relevant to anything.

Magicians Lewis October 1995. This looked like another wild goose chase, until I scrolled down near the bottom of the results page and saw a snippet of text: *blogger EoinDubh reports the magicians may have been in Lewis in the north of Scotland in Oct 1995.*

Clicking on the link, I found a treasure trove. It was a section from some kind of discussion forum, and seemed to have at least ten or twelve different contributors. Even more surprising was that Lewis barely merited a passing mention: the magicians, if indeed these were one and the same group, had been reported in places all over the continent. They had been sighted at Mont St. Michel in 1992, in Hungary in 1996, some small Turkish town in 1999. Some claimed that they had been in Estonia for the whole of the summer of 1989, although there was less consensus on this point.

Most of the night slipped away as I read through old postings, occasionally pulling an atlas from my bookshelf to refer to where some of these places were. I couldn't see any kind of pattern to it, apart from the fact that they all seemed to be small towns at the largest.

Eventually I made myself a sandwich and returned to my desk, compelled by the new story unfolding before my eyes. First the magicians had been a single anomaly, then there had been the two returns to Lewis; now they were a roving band that had been tracked through a dozen or more countries. Obviously, they had to have gone somewhere upon leaving the Western Isles, but I had never really given thought to where that might have been, nor that they would have performed elsewhere.

What was truly fascinating was the speculation on what determined their itinerary. There did not seem to be any one unifying factor. They had been seen near Avignon twice on the summer solstice, and in a coastal Norwegian village around the time of a peculiar tidal phenomenon. But other times, no one could point to anything out of the ordinary. The discussion was so lengthy that eventually I searched the page for the word 'Lewis'.

Here again was a shock: there had been another visit. Someone reported a grandparent's half-remembered story that seemed to fit, placing them back near Callanish in the late 1930s. No details, and no specific date, but still, it was another piece to this puzzle, the contours and size of which I didn't know.

It became a sort of hobby that I would return to every now and then, keeping up with the scattered, fragmented information on the magicians. Alan likened it to a scab that I couldn't help picking at, and part of me had to admit that it was an apt comparison. It never took over my life – despite Alan's occasional jokes to the contrary once he moved in with me – but it was definitely a thread that ran through it.

I eventually – not without some trepidation – shared what I knew about 1920 and 1957 with the online community, although I kept the details of Granny Chrissie's story to myself. There was a sort of common consent that no one divulged too many details of what, exactly, had been seen in the actual show. It just whetted my curiosity, this gnawing awareness that some of these people had seen the magicians for themselves – a few actually travelled around, with occasional success, based on their educated guesses on where the troupe might go next – and I had missed them by a matter of months. I was sure now that they would come back again to Lewis at some point in the future, but I had no idea when.

2011

CHAPTER TEN

The turning point was a posting of a scan of a newspaper article. It placed the magicians on Lewis yet again, this time in 1976 – the year after I was born. And, most astonishingly, it included a photo. I had been following the online discussion of the magicians for a decade, and there had never been a photo before.

I printed it out to pin up beside the heavily-annotated map of Europe that now took up most of the wall above my computer desk. The photo had been already old when it was scanned, and the reproduction had not done it any favours. But it showed an array of multicoloured tents on a field, just as Granny Chrissie had described. People were scattered around the tents – teenagers in jeans, older people dressed far more conservatively, young kids in woolly sweaters with patched knees on their trousers, one little one clutching some kind of stuffed toy. There wasn't much of the landscape visible, but I could fill in the surroundings in my mind's eye.

For some time after that, I was just excited to have photographic evidence. Granted, it was only of the tents – as far as I could tell, none of the actual magicians were pictured – but still, there truly was something to a picture that said more than words on a page could. It was several weeks later that it struck me: there was something of a pattern. Grabbing a pen and an old envelope – the closest paper to hand – I wrote them down.

1920

Late 1930s?

1957

1976

1995

It wasn't exactly every nineteen years, although I had thought so for a minute or two. Whatever date actually went with the 1930s visit, there were thirty-seven years, not thirty-eight, between Granny Chrissie's story and that of Margaret who I'd met on the airplane years before. But maybe it split the difference somehow. I revised the list.

June/July 1920

Late 1930s?

April 1957

1976 – what month?

October 1995

No, that only confused me more. I crossed it out and went back to the original. It was mostly nineteen-year intervals, though, give or take. Nineteen was a number that I couldn't see any significance to, but it didn't hurt to look it up. I tried *Isle of Lewis every 19 years*, not hoping for much.

But there was a result, and it referenced Callanish. I had no idea where they got their information from, but about three-quarters of the way down their write-up there were a couple of paragraphs about the possible ritual uses of the standing stones.

What grabbed me were two sentences:

> *Some astronomers have suggested that the monument was oriented towards the line of hills, sometimes known as the 'Sleeping Beauty', where the moon skipped along the horizon every 18 or 19 years. In the northern hemisphere, this phenomenon only occurs at this particular latitude (58 degrees).*

I had no idea what they meant by the moon skipping along the horizon, or why it would only happen at 58 degrees north – nor did I care. And what the magicians could possibly want with such a phenomenon was just as much a mystery. But it was something that happened at Callanish – and at not too many other places in the world – and it fit the pattern. Every eighteen or nineteen years: it even made sense of the slight irregularity to the pattern.

It became my mission for a while, to try and figure out if the moon-skipping event actually lined up with the dates I had for the magicians, but to no avail. I couldn't even find any other mention of its existence, let alone a more detailed description or a proper name.

Around the end of 2011, I finally did the math.

If my theory was correct, the magicians should be coming back in 2013 or 2014.

A year or two or three would have seemed like a world away when I'd been twenty, but now, not so much. It was still just something that percolated in the background in my free time, a weird sort of hobby, but now I had a deadline. A maddeningly vague one, to be sure, but a deadline.

2012

CHAPTER ELEVEN

"I've had the worst day," I announced, as I let myself into the house. "Remember when I was worried they were going to lay people off, and you told me I was crazy? I told you so. Alan?" I added, realizing that no one had responded.

Strange. I was a bit late, granted – a few of us had gone for a drink after receiving the bad news – and I wouldn't have been surprised if Alan had gone ahead and eaten without me, but it wasn't like him to go out without saying anything. He worked from home and was usually glad of some company by the time I got in.

It was only belatedly that I thought to check my phone. Sure enough, there was a text from him, sent mid-afternoon: *Have to go see a client, kind of emergency. Go ahead with dinner, might be pretty late.*

What timing. Tossing my bag onto the couch, I headed upstairs to change out of my work clothes. I could see from the open closet doors and the jeans on the floor that this must have been an important enough client to require dressing up; unusual, definitely, though not unheard of.

It was only on the way back out of the room that I noticed his wedding ring left behind on the bedside table. Not a business meeting at all, then.

Thus, at the age of thirty-seven, I suddenly found myself not only jobless, but single, my formerly pleasant life falling in around me in one fell swoop as I uncovered the sordid details of just how thoroughly – and for how long – Alan had betrayed my trust. While I went about remedying the employment situation as soon as possible, I still found myself with spare time on my hands and thoughts in my head that I didn't want to entertain – and 2013, at least, was around the corner. I seized on the idea of the magicians with renewed energy, conscious though I was that it was the very definition of escapism.

Still, no further information was forthcoming that might give me any idea when to expect the magicians to turn up on Lewis. I was going to have to do this the old-fashioned way and take it to the experts; looking up my old university's astronomy department, I emailed all the faculty and graduate students whose listed research fields seemed like they might include the moon.

I apologize for troubling you with a layperson's question, but I am trying to find out more about a phenomenon that apparently occurs every 18 or 19 years at 58 degrees north latitude, where the moon appears to skip across the horizon. I believe this will occur next in 2013 or 2014, but as I don't know the proper name for it, I haven't been able to pin down the date. I was hoping you might be able to help me.

Into the ether went a dozen or so messages, to which I didn't honestly expect an answer. However, a couple of weeks later, I found a reply in my inbox.

Hi Heather, sorry it has taken me a while as I'm working on my comprehensive exams, it began. There followed a rather lengthy scientific explanation, complete with references to books and journals, which I skimmed over. Towards the end, I saw it: *The next time it should be visible – weather permitting – would be August 21, 2013.*

And so, at last, I had an agenda. It gave me time to save

money, get my legal matters dealt with, and plan work and finances around taking a large chunk of time off to travel. The one thing I had not figured out was what, exactly, I expected to happen. I was basing a great deal on some educated guesswork, but in the worst-case scenario, I had not had a vacation in a long time. In the best case, I still had no idea what I would do.

2013

CHAPTER TWELVE

I opened my door to find my sister there, with a bakery box in her hands. "Congratulations!"

"Is that really what I think it is?" I asked, raising an eyebrow at the ribbon-tied box as she came into the house and set it on my kitchen counter. Sure enough, when I got the scissors and opened it up, there it was, in lurid red letters on the chocolate icing: HAPPY DIVORCE!

"Too soon?" she asked.

"Well, the papers have only been finalized for three days…" I began, but then relented. "No, it's cool. Good riddance to bad rubbish, right?" The truth was, I had thought that Alan was the love of my life. We'd been married for eight years, and dating for three before that, and until the very end, when he'd gotten careless, I'd had no idea that he had been sleeping with a revolving door of other women for virtually the whole time we'd been together.

"Scumbag," she agreed. "So, what are you going to do now?"

"Eat a piece of cake. Then leave the country."

"Seriously? You're really going?"

"Why not?" I had been tempted to flee somewhere far, far away from the moment I had confronted Alan and kicked him out of the house – out of my house. But first there had been the possessions to divide, and the job hunt to tackle, and the divorce proceedings to initiate. But that was all done now; the papers were in hand, I had gone back to my maiden name, and my current work contract was winding up at the end of the next month. "I've got time, and I've got money. Well, you know, not a lot of money, but enough to go away for a while. I'm at a crossroads; I need a change of scenery." It wasn't just that, of course, but I could hardly tell her the real reason.

As I said it, my eyes wandered to the framed poster above the dining room table – a print of the Callanish Stones, dramatically silhouetted against a sunset sky. I'd brought it home as a souvenir seventeen years ago – how was it possible, that it had been seventeen years? But if there was ever a time to take a chance and go back, it was now.

CHAPTER THIRTEEN

I had given myself plenty of time, I hoped. My flight departed Toronto on the 27th of July, and I arrived in Edinburgh the following morning to a bright, high overcast day, already very light despite the early hour. Just breathing in the air, I noticed subtle differences from what I was used to at home. It already made me feel as if I were closer to the magicians, but I tried to put that thought aside; I could still be completely wrong about all of it.

My plan was to spend my first few days in the capital before heading to the islands. I had fallen in love with Edinburgh on my university trip and its charms had not lessened with the passage of years. On my third night there, the sounds of lively fiddle music drew me into a small pub just off the Royal Mile. Once inside the door it was practically wall-to-wall people, and it took me a while to make my way towards the bar. A man noticed me trying to work my way through, and waved the barman over on my behalf.

"Thanks," I said, before giving my order. "It's nuts in here."

"I know. Not even room to take my jacket off," he replied, looking pleased about it. "They're good players. I was just glad to get in the door."

His accent was familiar – not home, exactly, but definitely that side of the pond. I actually debated a minute before asking; after

Alan, I was still struggling not to view men as the enemy, but there was something about the stranger's body language that put me at ease. "Are you American or Canadian?"

The man chuckled, though I saw it more than heard it. "I get that sometimes. I'm from Buffalo, originally, which I guess is about as close as you get to being both. Haven't lived in the States for a while now, though. You're Canadian, or you wouldn't have asked."

I nodded. "Toronto." Kitchener didn't bear explaining.

The musicians began another song at that point, and I might have moved away with my drink, except that there was really nowhere else to move. And so I listened with the stranger from Buffalo, until there was another break.

"What are you doing in Scotland?"

I shrugged. "Partly just visiting; I haven't been away in a long time. But mostly… well, maybe a wild goose chase, although I hope not. It's kind of a long story," I added, wondering what had possessed me to spout nonsense in response to a simple question.

But the stranger just smiled. "I'm sure it is. I hope you find what you're looking for. Have you been here before?"

"Once," I replied, having to lean in a bit to be heard. "When I was still in university. That was in the spring, so things weren't quite as busy as this."

"If you want to see busy, you should come back here in a week or two, when the Festival's on. Performances in the streets, all kinds of stuff going on."

"Well, maybe if things do turn out to be a wild goose chase, I'll come back," I said.

The man motioned to the bartender for another drink; he offered me one as well, but I felt it best to decline. "I always try to get to Edinburgh for the Festival," he said. "I've got business elsewhere this year, though."

We chatted a bit about other places in Scotland, until it became apparent that the music was actually done for the night, and the bell rang for last call. I said goodnight, and headed out. It was only when I was halfway back to my hotel that it occurred to me that we'd never introduced ourselves, but it had been a pleasant evening, at any rate.

The next morning, I began my journey north, stopping overnight at Inverness. I had thought about coming to Lewis by another way – maybe going through the Isle of Skye and taking the ferry to Harris – but there was something that made me want to retrace my steps from seventeen years before, and come in to Stornoway directly.

Unlike my last journey, it appeared the weather was on my side; the clouds were breaking up and blowing away to the east, revealing increasing patches of bright blue sky. Once I reached the port at Ullapool and boarded the huge ferry, I spent some time trying to capture the hills and the sea in photos, though I knew I would not do them justice. As we pulled away from the mainland, I thought back to those old news clippings I'd read in the Stornoway library, so many years before. The magicians had arrived by sea in those days. I assumed they still would – the only other option was to fly in, after all – but it was strange to imagine. They might have walked these very same decks.

It was still warm in the sunshine, but the wind picked up as we left the shelter of the bay, sending most of the passengers inside to the comfort of the cafeteria or the lounge. There were only a handful of people left outside, sitting on benches or standing at the rail. I got a shock when I recognized one of them.

Thinking that it would be a strange coincidence, I looked again. Tall, leather jacket, hair a bit overdue for a trim: the friendly stranger from Buffalo. While I was debating whether it would be more awkward to go and initiate a conversation or pretend that I had not seen him, he turned and waved. It seemed the decision was made for me.

"How goes the wild goose chase?" he asked as I approached.

I held my hands out, palms up. "That remains to be seen."

"Indeed." With a grin, he tried to push his hair back out of his eyes, before giving up to the inevitability of the wind and turning a bit to face into it. "The Western Isles are an excellent place to go looking for things. Are you staying long?"

"It depends, I guess." I didn't want to elaborate too far, partly in case he had any ideas about asking me out – he seemed likeable, and was certainly not bad-looking, but I hadn't decided yet if I ever wanted a date again, let alone right now – but mostly because I didn't want to say too much and wind up sounding like a nut case. "I'm Heather, by the way."

He nodded, as if making a mental note of it, then shook my hand. "Eric. Eric Heyward. It's good to meet you properly, Heather. So, are you… from Lewis? Your family, I mean."

That, at least, was a safe topic. I explained about Leurbost, and Stornoway, and Archie and Chrissie sailing with the Metagama, and left out anything that was too odd-sounding. Eric seemed surprisingly interested in all of it; I was tempted to ask if he was some kind of historian, but was too busy answering his many questions. No, I didn't know too much about my family history earlier than that, except that Granny Chrissie had been a 'surprise baby', born long after her older brothers and the only girl of eight children. That, and that her parents had been Angus and Jessie Morrison. Yes, I had been to Leurbost; no, the family home wasn't still standing. My great-grandparents had emigrated in 1923; no, they hadn't had any children yet when they left. Yes, they had been quite young when they emigrated. 1902, both born in 1902. No, none of the rest of my family had any Lewis connections, so far as I knew; my dad's dad had been from Glasgow and no one knew much else about that branch, and then my mum's family were from the south of England and then France before that.

"What about you?" I finally managed to inquire. "I've been monopolizing the conversation here. Is your family from Lewis as well?" Perhaps he was trying to figure out if we were distant cousins.

Eric shook his head. "Nah. English and Irish, I guess, but my family's been in the USA for a couple hundred years. A lot of them have never left. Makes me a bit of a black sheep," he added, laughing.

I was about to say that he didn't look like one, but refrained; I didn't want to sound like I was trying to flirt, and besides, on second glance, it wasn't entirely true. While he had a nice amiable smile, there was something mischievous in his eyes that I couldn't quite put my finger on. Instead I asked, "Do you live in Scotland, then?"

He waved his hand vaguely. "I... travel a lot. There's a flat outside London where I keep my stuff, but I don't know that I've really belonged to anywhere for a while now. There's places I feel more connected to than others, but I try not to get too caught up in whether I have an address there or not."

They sounded like words I would have expected from someone else. He was about my own age, I guessed, mid-thirties or so: too young to be an old hippie, but didn't look the part of a new-age philosopher type, either. I wondered what he did for a living, but didn't like to ask that question of people as a general rule. Before I could think of anything else to ask, though, his phone rang. With an apologetic smile, he excused himself, walking slowly away as he talked.

I thought he might come back and resume our conversation, but when fifteen or twenty minutes passed, I dismissed it. In any case, Lewis was looming larger in front of me now – so different from my last arrival, when I'd hardly been able to see twenty feet through the fog – and I felt my nerves rising as we drew closer.

This was August the first, and if my theories were actually correct – and I knew all too well that this was still a big 'if' – the magicians would want to be at Callanish to see the moon's strange alignment on the twenty-first. Three weeks. If they did come, I had no idea how far in advance it might be; reports of their comings and goings in other places varied widely on this; even in Lewis specifically, it seemed that they had stayed anywhere from a few days to nearly a month in the past. They might be there already, for all I knew.

CHAPTER FOURTEEN

I had booked a small cottage in Callanish for most of my stay, but my first night would be in Stornoway. And even before dropping my bag off at the hotel, my first action on setting foot on the island was to double-check every notice, bill and poster I passed, looking for any evidence that the magicians might already be on the island. There was none to be found. I wasn't sure if I was disappointed or relieved – my biggest fear, even more than the possibility that they might not come, was that I might once again have narrowly missed them. With that question answered at least, I stopped to check in at my hotel and took advantage of the free wi-fi in the room to check for any news of my quarry.

The magicians had been seen near Glastonbury at the summer solstice, and not since then. Glastonbury was down in the south of England – not far away in the grand scheme of things, though that might not mean anything at all. I had been second-guessing myself since the moment I had first booked the trip, and it was going into overdrive now. But there was no turning back.

The next day was rainy and I was not due in Callanish till late afternoon, so I stayed in town and headed to the local arts centre. I watched a short film in Gaelic – thankfully with English subtitles –

in the cinema, and was wandering through a photo exhibit in the gallery afterwards when I heard a familiar voice. Eric Heyward was looking at a large photo on the opposite wall and talking to the gallery attendant. This time I didn't feel quite as strange about running into him.

"My great-great-grandparents were crofters," I said by way of greeting, referring to the subject of the photographs. "The clothes are different, and he's probably got wi-fi and satellite TV in his house, but I guess some things don't change so much."

Both of them turned to look at me. The attendant engaged me in some pleasant conversation about my family roots for a while, but Eric merely observed until the young woman went off to speak with another visitor. "Getting in touch with your roots, or just getting out of the rain?"

"A bit of both," I admitted. "I didn't know what the exhibit was till I came in."

"Any luck yet on the wild goose chase?" This time he was definitely amused; I didn't think it was at my expense, but I couldn't be sure.

"I wouldn't be spending the morning here if that was the case," I replied, keeping my tone noncommittal. "But I haven't given up hope just yet."

"Good. Listen, do you want to get a coffee or something?" He tilted his head, apparently reading my hesitation. "Or maybe another time? I'll be here for a while," he continued, looking neither surprised nor offended. Before I could respond, a bell sounded; he pulled his phone out of his pocket and glanced at it. "Actually, it turns out I've got to run. Let me know if you want a rain check on that coffee." The grin returned in full force. "I think I might be able to help you find what you're looking for."

It was just straddling the line of being too cocky, and I was already thinking that I would not be taking him up on it, friendly though he was, even as he was pulling a card out of his pocket and writing something on the back of it. He shook my hand, and popped his card halfway into the top pocket of my jacket. "It was nice seeing you, Heather. I have a feeling we'll run into each other again soon."

I watched as he walked out of the gallery and past the front window: still smiling, but walking with purpose, presumably on his way to something important. It was only after he was out of sight that it occurred to me to actually look at the card.

Heavy cardstock, good quality, a rich cream colour. I had pulled it out so that I saw the reverse first; in precise block capitals, like a draftsman's, it said *An Drochaid Farm, Callanish.*

For a moment, I just thought what a coincidence it was that he was staying near Callanish as well, and then out of nowhere, another idea struck me. It couldn't possibly be – and yet I had broken out in goose bumps and the bottom had dropped mysteriously out of my stomach, and I still hadn't turned the card over to see the front. Perhaps ten seconds passed, but it felt like an hour, before I convinced myself to flip it over.

And there it was.

The font was as familiar to me as the back of my hand, and I could hear Granny Chrissie's voice in my head, reciting what I was now reading.

A troupe of MAGICIANS from parts unknown – Nightly performances to astound and amaze!

I ran out of the gallery, heedless of the surprised glances of the other patrons, into the street in the vain hope of catching up with Eric Heyward, originally from Buffalo, New York. It seemed I had met – three times! – with one of the magicians I had been fixated on for twenty-five years, and not realized it.

He was gone, of course.

CHAPTER FIFTEEN

I stood there on the empty sidewalk in the rain, not knowing what to do. My first instinct was to go to Callanish immediately, by the first means of transport available, but within a minute or two I was able to find a few flaws in that plan. The main one was that I wasn't sure that they were actually there yet. Eric had seemed at loose ends, or at least not in any particular hurry to be anywhere, until he had received that text in the gallery. Perhaps they were all arriving separately, and it had been one – or all? – of the others that he had taken off to meet. They would have to get themselves to Callanish to begin with, and then they would have to get things set up. I was not likely to miss the whole thing by waiting for the four o'clock bus.

That left me a couple of hours to check out of my hotel, buy a few groceries, withdraw some cash, and head for the bus station. I was still a little early, and found myself scanning every passer-by, conscious that any one of them could potentially be one of the magicians; Eric had not looked particularly out of the ordinary, after all.

The bus was not terribly busy. It was late in the day for tourists to be heading to the standing stones, and most of the passengers seemed to be elderly ladies on their way home with their shopping. One of them smiled at me and my grocery bags, and greeted me in Gaelic. I managed to reply with "Feasgar math" – good afternoon – one of the small handful of phrases I had taught myself in anticipation of the trip.

Virtually everything in Stornoway was labelled in both languages, and I had heard Gaelic used in official announcements on the ferry, but this was my first time really encountering it as an everyday language, and I listened with interest as the two ladies behind me on the bus chatted away. The conversation seemed to take an animated turn, with one woman reacting with obvious disbelief to what her seatmate was telling her. I presumed it was some kind of small-town gossip; all I knew was there was somebody or something called 'drooyen' being mentioned a lot, and other passengers were being drawn into the conversation.

My ears perked up when I realized there was some English in the mix as well, mainly numbers – but it was hearing 'ninety-five' and 'seventy-six' that made me rummage into my bag for the little Gaelic dictionary I'd picked up on a whim in Inverness. Flipping to the English end, I found it:

Magic *adj. draoidheil; n. draoidheachd.*
Magician *n. draoidh m.; pl. draoidhean.*

Just to be sure, I looked in the other half of the book.

Draoidh *m. druid; magician.*

The word was spreading. The magicians had come.

CHAPTER SIXTEEN

As soon as the bus drew nearer to Callanish, I gave up eavesdropping and started scanning the horizon in all directions, looking for any hint of tents. I had no idea whether the houses and farms were numbered in any kind of sequential order – I certainly hadn't seen many numbers, just occasional house names on gates – and I wasn't sure whether we might pass An Drochaid Farm on the way to my stop. The owner of the cottage had told me to get off at the Callanish post office, which was the next stop after the standing stones; one of the elderly Gaelic-speaking ladies stepped down from the bus there as well.

I had directions, but I was keen to talk to someone; I assumed she must speak English as well. "Excuse me, is this the right way to Kestrel Cottage?" I asked, pointing up the tiny single-track road.

"Just there," she replied, her accent soft and smooth like a tumbled stone out of the water. "We've actually just passed it; you could have asked the driver to stop right at the lane if you'd known. Follow back along the road and look out for the yellow flowers at the laneway, just by the cattle grid. You'll be here to visit the standing stones?"

It was time to tip my hand. "Actually, I'm here to see the magicians." I showed her the card from my pocket. "Is this farm close by?"

She peered closely at the card, pushing her glasses up the bridge of her nose. "Ah, so it's true, then; they have come back. I thought it must be getting about near their time."

"You've seen them before?" She seemed to be going the same way as me, so I moderated my pace to hers.

"Almost every time," she said, with a hint of pride. "I first saw them when I was just a wee girl. The only time I missed them was 'fifty-seven, when I was in hospital – I had twins, you see, and they had to have me in the hospital in town for a month. To think nowadays they turn you out almost as soon as you've had the baby!" She shook her head. "How did you hear about the magicians? I'd always thought they were our own little island secret."

"My great-grandmother came from Leurbost. She saw them in nineteen-twenty," I explained.

"Well, that's before my time, but oh, I heard whispers about it, years later. So many of the young men lost in the war, or away with the fishing fleet, you see." When it became apparent that I did not quite get the connection, she elaborated. "And all the young girls going to the magic show, with stars in their eyes... well. I'm sure your great-gran didn't get involved with any of that," she hastened to add.

I thought of Chrissie and Raffaele, and wondered just how far their romance had gone. "She did get married the next year," I said, already calculating that she would have had to marry my great-granddad quite a lot sooner if she'd had any fears in that direction. "They didn't have their first child till a couple of years later, though, just after they got to Canada."

"Of course," she replied, then motioned to a house on our left. "Here's my place; I'd best be in and get my shopping away before my grandsons come by. Kestrel Cottage is just down the way, on the opposite side. Oh! And I never did tell you where the farm is. It's just down there, on the other road – you can't quite see it from here. They may not be there yet; I didn't think I spied anything when we passed by the side of there on the bus, though I didn't know to look. If you walk just a wee bit past your door and look down that way, you'll see if the tents are going up."

We had been lingering at her front gate for a minute or so while she finished explaining this. "I'm sure I'll see you there, before long," she continued. "I'm glad I've been spared to see them one more time, since I'm eighty-three now. And feel free to stop in for a cup of tea any time you see my lights on. I'm Flora Nicolson, by the way."

"Heather Ross," I replied. "Thanks so much."

"Did your great-gran marry a Ross, then? There were Rosses at Leurbost, I think."

I shook my head. "No, she married a MacDonald. My gran – her daughter – married a Ross, but from Glasgow."

"Hmm. Well, I should get on, and let you do the same. I'll be seeing you."

Walking more quickly now, I covered the remaining hundred yards or so to the door of Kestrel Cottage. As promised, the owner was waiting there to show me around and leave me with the key. Almost as soon as she was gone, I dashed back out to the road and went a little further past the house, just as Flora had suggested; there was a slight rise here that gave a greater view around.

The first thing that struck me was just how close the standing stones were. But turning to the left and scanning down the gentle slope, all I saw there across the field was a widely-spaced row of houses, strung out along a narrow road much like the one I stood on. I looked at Eric's card again; it was the real thing, and the right place, so perhaps I had just beaten them to it.

I went back inside and had a better look around the cottage; it was small, but generous enough for just one person. I put my food away properly, tossed my other bags into the larger of the two bedrooms, and went out again to see if anything was going on down the road. This time, I could see a pair of vans turning off into a laneway; both were white and fairly nondescript, but perhaps this was something. I went a few steps closer, leaned on a low stone wall, and waited.

For a while, there was nothing to see except a number of people going to and fro; the other road was probably half a kilometre away, and so I couldn't make out any detail. This was useless. If the tents went up I would certainly be able to see that from here, but in the meantime, there was nothing to be gained from staring at an empty field. Part of me didn't want to see it all until it was ready, either; instead, since it was so close by, I walked over to the stone circle.

It felt funny to come in by the back gate, but I knew from my last visit that there was no admission charge. At nearly six o'clock, the sun was still well up in the western sky, peeking now and then through bands of grey cloud; we were several weeks past the solstice, but it had been staying light till well past nine in the evening. After taking my time viewing each of the stones up close, I was just debating whether to head back to the cottage and cook myself some dinner, when a horn sounded.

Definitely not a car horn: it was something more musical, though it was just one lingering note echoing over the landscape, and unusual enough that I was not the only person who had stopped in their tracks to look around. But as the other people resumed their activity, I headed for the back gate. I was sure that the sound had come from the general direction of that field on the lower road. Once clear of the gate, I started to jog, until I got to the bend in the road where I could see down the slope.

They were here.

It had only been an hour, at the absolute most, since I had walked away from this spot, and in that time the field had been entirely filled in with an array of tents in every size and colour imaginable. Pennants flew from the tops of the marquees, and as the sun broke through to cast a slanting golden light over the scene, I thought it looked more like a medieval encampment than a circus.

Nightly performances, the card said. It was time.

CHAPTER SEVENTEEN

There were only a few others walking down the little road in that direction, and one or two cars passing; clearly, word of the magicians' arrival had not yet reached far and wide. Two white vans were not exactly the gaudy wagon Auntie Chrissie had described to me, after all. But this being the twenty-first century, I had no doubt their presence would soon be public knowledge.

Music was filtering past on the breeze, becoming clearer as I grew closer. The walk was scarcely more than ten minutes, but I was conscious of each step drawing me nearer; I had not been this nervous for anything in many years.

There was a faded sign at the gate that read *An Drochaid*, and the house looked as if it hadn't been lived in in a few years. Beyond the house, though, I could hear the music and see a flicker of lights against the clouds. And then I stepped into the lane, and there it was.

An archway, outlined in the tiniest white lights, stood where the backyard of the house gave way to open field. Just beyond it was a small ticket booth, and inside was a woman of completely indeterminate age, with huge dark eyes and the most fantastic silver-white hair. "How much is it?" I asked her.

"Ten pounds, my dearie," she replied. After taking the note I gave her, she reached for my hand and drew a symbol on it. The ink glowed at first, then disappeared after I removed my hand from the counter. "Are you all right?" It was only when she asked the question that I realized that I had just been standing there for a minute, hesitant to take the final step.

"Yes. Yes, of course," I replied, hoping I was managing to smile. I was happy, nervous, overwhelmed, and I hadn't even stepped into a tent yet. With a deep breath, I moved past the ticket kiosk and into the magicians' domain.

People wandered here and there, some with a clear destination and others ambling, trying to decide. I thought of Granny Chrissie and the dark blue tent, but if that still existed, I didn't feel ready for it. Perhaps it would be better to start in one of the larger ones, where I would not be alone.

The largest of all was striped red and gold, with three peaks each bearing a different-coloured pennant. It was as good a starting point as any. I was expecting something like bleachers or circus rings inside, but I supposed I should have known better. The tent's opening was veiled with several layers of sheer red and gold cloth, so that the interior was only gradually revealed: a space lit with hanging lanterns that swayed gently back and forth, casting warm glows and unpredictable moving shadows. In some places, more of the gauzy fabric hung down, almost dividing the area into rooms.

Cushions lay scattered on the ground; a few children sprawled out on them, their parents sitting more primly, all watching a woman on a chaise longue as she stroked her hand down the multicoloured plumage of a parrot. Before my eyes the bird turned silver, then blue. A man walked by with a massive snake coiled round his neck; it slithered down his arm to the ground and moved towards me. I gasped, and stepped back, but with a flick of his wrist the python became merely a snakeskin-print scarf, which he wound back up in one hand. From his balled-up fist, a snake reappeared and resumed its place around the man's shoulders.

"It's the Menagerie," came a soft voice at my shoulder, and I turned to see Flora Nicolson dressed up for the occasion. "The tent was different last time, but oh, I do so love the tricks with the animals. Oh my, it's Johannes with the tiger," she exclaimed. "He doesn't look a day older than when I last saw him."

Indeed, from behind a scrim halfway down the tent, a dark-haired man maybe my father's age came walking with a massive tiger, which did not appear to be restrained in any way that I could see. I wondered if it was the man or the animal, or both, who had not aged since their last visit. But before I could ask, Flora was on her way across the tent to speak to him; it appeared that he remembered her, for they talked for a few minutes, the tiger prowling idly in figure-eights around their conversation.

The animal made me uneasy, and fascinated me at the same time. Parrots and even snakes were one thing, but you couldn't just travel around with a tiger, no matter how strange you were. They couldn't have brought a tiger here in a van, or transported one on the ferry. And yet all the evidence of my senses told me that this was a real, live, possibly very dangerous, actual tiger. Against my better judgment, I moved closer. Flora and Johannes were still chatting; the big cat glanced once in my direction but did not change its repetitive path. From two feet away, I could not see any evidence that it was a trick.

"It's quite alright," Johannes said to me, without really looking my way. "You can touch her."

I had not waited this long or come this far to be a coward. Steeling my nerves to pretend that she was a large friendly dog, I held out my closed fist for the tiger to sniff. She looked at me again as she twisted round her master's legs, but ignored my hand. On her next pass, I took a deep breath and reached to touch her back.

The animal was solid: thick fur over muscle. And then she was not. Like sand running through my fingers, the beast became less and less tangible, completely disappearing by the time my hand should have reached her tail. Shocked, I looked to the magician, Johannes, for some confirmation of what I had just experienced –

only to see him fade elegantly into the ether as well.

"What was…?" I trailed off, not sure what I wanted to ask. "Was that real?"

Flora smiled and patted my arm. "Oh, you'll give yourself a headache if you ask that question too often here, love. But it is a bit startling, the first time. Johannes is so very talented, isn't he?" When I continued to stare, slightly open-mouthed, at the space where they had been, she went on. "Johannes is real; he's one of the best. I think the tiger is an illusion, but I've never been just absolutely sure."

With those words of reassurance, she pottered off down the tent towards what looked like a swarm of glittering dragonflies. Still uncertain how I felt about the tiger, I decided to leave the Menagerie and see what the other tents might hold.

I had been inside longer than I'd thought; the sun was setting now, making the lights on and around the tents stand out brighter. More people had arrived, although it was still by no means crowded, and there seemed to be a bit of a queue forming outside a long, narrow tent that was pale at the top, deepening to a rich orange hue close to the ground. Intrigued, I fell in behind a couple of young men. "Do you know what this one is?" I asked.

The shorter of the pair turned to reply. "I think it's food. I smell chips from somewhere, anyway."

"That's never chips," his companion put in. "It's curry or something."

Wrinkling my nose, I sniffed the air. Now that they mentioned it, I did notice a distinct foody aroma that seemed to be coming from this tent, but I had no idea what they were talking about; I wasn't sure what it was, but it reminded me of wood smoke and gingerbread. I was so busy trying to identify it that I nearly missed the fact that the line had moved on ahead of me, leaving me standing outside the tent on my own.

When I stepped in, it was to such a swirl of smells and sights that I was taken aback. The whole length of the tent was a stretch of tables, all laden with silver platters of food, much of which I was at a loss to identify. One of the nearest held a staggering pyramid of sweets, powdered sugar dusted over a rainbow of translucent cubes. I picked one up and looked at it more closely, and then hesitated. I had just seen a parrot turn colours and a tiger disappear – what might the food do, in a place like this?

"I like the purple ones, myself," came a voice at my shoulder. I turned to see Eric beside me, looking much the same as he had that morning. Had it really been less than a day? It was hard to believe. He reached past me and picked up one of the larger sweets. "I think they're pomegranate." When he realized that I was still standing there with a candy in my palm, he laughed. "It's just food, Heather. It's not going to burst into flames or turn you into a frog."

I turned it over in my hand. Turkish Delight, of all things. "I don't know. I've read the Narnia books."

Still chuckling, he took it from me and popped it into his mouth. "If I can paraphrase, sometimes a candy is just a candy. But I'd better go; I should have been ready by now. Look for the green tent a bit later."

Slipping past me, he leaned across a table further down and took a silver bottle and what looked like a sandwich, then ducked out through some unseen side flap of the tent. It was only when he was gone that I was struck by all my unasked questions. He looked so normal; I still could not quite believe that he was a part of all this.

I took another piece of the Turkish Delight, and this time, I tasted it.

CHAPTER EIGHTEEN

As it descended into full dark, the field took on a new appearance with the mix of light and shadow. The areas that were well-lit were a carnival, but there were many dimmer alleys and corners as well. Some of the tents glowed from within rather than bearing lights on the exterior, others glittered faintly with symbols I did not understand. There was one laneway where I found my footsteps sparking some kind of luminescent trail on the rough ground. In the darker areas, I was keenly aware of the distinction between moonlight and cloud cover; other than the lit-up windows of a few faraway houses, there was little else in the way of illumination from the surrounding area.

There were at least three different shades of green among the many tents, and I saw amazing things in each of them, but of Eric Heyward there was no sign. I was beginning to question my assumption about him; perhaps he wasn't one of the magicians, after all, but simply a follower of theirs? I knew there were people who tried their best to track the troupe across Europe, presumably using the same sort of guesswork I had employed. Maybe he was passing along a card he'd been given. It seemed, on the surface, to be a more logical explanation – after all, everyone said that the magicians disappeared without a trace in between shows, not that they hung about in touristy Edinburgh pubs.

Even so, he clearly knew more about the magicians than I did; I would have liked to have had him show me around. The field that had looked so small when it was empty – certainly not big enough to be called a 'farm' by any of my reckoning – now felt like an enormous expanse; I had no idea how many tents I had already seen, and I was sure that I had barely scratched the surface.

Coming around a corner in one of the darker areas of the field, I found a tent that was illuminated in the most curious manner yet. A light from somewhere – I was sure it was coming from outside, not inside, but couldn't place its source – was cycling from bright to dark and back again, as if someone was using a dimmer switch. At the darkest, the tent nearly disappeared into the night; at the brightest I was just able to pick out that the sides of it were not black, as I had first supposed, but a deep emerald. Yet another hue of green. There was no sound from inside it, no strange smell to pique my curiosity, and I saw no one else around. There was only this strange, unidentifiable light.

I went in.

Many of the tents had seemed larger on the inside than they had looked from the outside, and this was no exception. It was hard to tell exactly how large I thought it was, though, because the interior was nearly filled with a swirling, pearl-grey mist that was spilling down from a point near the tent's peak. Through gaps in the fog, I could just make out that there were people seated in a ring around the perimeter; I found an empty spot on the curving wooden bench and waited, not sure what I was waiting for.

The mist blew around a little each time another person opened the tent flap and came in, but for five or even ten minutes, that was all that happened, although I could feel an air of anticipation charging the space. And then there was a sound, so low that I felt it more than heard it, like a string plucked on some instrument lower than a bass. It sent a visible shudder through the mist and called everyone to attention.

A change spread through the fog then, as if someone had spilled in drops of food colouring. A deep green almost like the silks of the tent, then blue. It was taking shape now, becoming a landscape that wavered with each puff of air. A drop of pure black became a raven, that detached itself from the mass of mist, taking on a three-dimensional form as it flew around the ring of seats, dipping so low over my head that I felt a caress of cool, damp air as it passed by. The single raven became a flock, swooping and diving through the tent, eliciting shrieks of surprise from some of the audience.

Following them came a pure white bird, larger, swifter, that swallowed the ravens whole. After that, it opened its great beak and began to consume the fog, till it was the only thing left in the centre of the ring. Then, it dissolved, leaving behind the figure of a man. It was only as the final wisps of mist left the air that I realized that this last was no illusion, but an actual breathing human, all in black. He faced the opposite side of the tent, his head down, one hand behind his back.

The audience burst out into applause, doubly so as he bowed deeply to that side of the room. He spun round and did the same again, this time facing in my direction; it was only then that I recognized him in the dim light. Eric Heyward. He met my eyes then, and gave just a flash of a grin, before giving one more bow and leaving the tent.

Cheers and clapping continued for a minute or two, but when it became apparent that the performance was over, people started slowly, reluctantly, to move on. I followed them out into the night and circled round the outside of the tent. It was in darkness now, the light show over, and there was no sign of Eric. Presuming he was preparing for another performance, I went on my way.

After two more tents, I looked at my watch for the first time since leaving the cottage and was astonished to see that it was after four, nearly morning; the eastern sky was no longer quite fully black, and there was a bird beginning to sing somewhere. I had been awake for the best part of twenty hours and hadn't thought of it, but with the realization of the lateness of the hour I felt suddenly tired. Although I was afraid of missing a thing, I could see that the coming of dawn was also heralding the close of the show, at least for the night. With one more look across the field, I slipped out through the gateway and down the dark road, trying to understand everything that I had seen.

CHAPTER NINETEEN

After all the night's events, I expected not to sleep at all. But the quiet cottage, the comfortable bed, and the sheer weight of having been awake for so long caught up with me almost as soon as my head hit the pillow. I woke up well after ten, confused for a moment before I remembered where I was.

It hadn't been a dream. If I'd needed reassurance of that fact, there was the magicians' card on the bedside table, and my jeans hanging over the chair still visibly smudged with powdered sugar from the Turkish Delight. I knew it had all been real – well, to the extent that vanishing wild cats and figures of mist could be counted as real – and yet I still felt compelled, the moment I was dressed, to walk the stone's throw down the road to see for myself that the tents were still there.

They were. The scene was less vivid now, unlit under a dull grey sky, the wind blowing spatters of rain nearly sideways into my eyes, but it was all still there. I could see a single figure walk between two tents, dark head bowed against the weather. I wondered where the magicians were staying – not in the tents, surely – and if the show would go on should the weather take a turn for the worse.

A fresh gust of wind drove me back into the cottage to make

a belated breakfast, after which I debated what to do with the day. The card advertised nightly performances, and I assumed that was to be taken literally; I did not expect to see the field down the slope come back to life till late afternoon at the earliest. The weather did not invite hiking or sightseeing, and it was Saturday. Remembering how strictly Lewis rolled up its sidewalks in observance of the sabbath, I headed back on the bus into Stornoway to get more groceries.

While the bus was pulled over to take on passengers at Achmore, a van drove slowly past. It would have been wholly unremarkable if not for the banner on its side. In red, gold and silver, it presented a technicolour version of the understated card I carried in my pocket. I wasn't the only one to notice; the handful of passengers on the bus were suddenly all talking at once, in both English and Gaelic.

Tha na draoidhean air tilleadh. The magicians have returned.

No doubt there would be many more people at the performances this evening. I pulled the bus timetable from my pocket, wondering what time I would be able to make it back; coming from a big city, the one thing I found rather difficult about such a remote island was the infrequency of any kind of transit. After the previous night, I did not want to miss a minute.

In any case, I managed to get my shopping done, and in the checkout line I ran into Flora Nicolson again. "We have to stop meeting like this," I joked.

She laughed. "I'm not usually doing my messages at this time of day, but I was away out till some hour last night. I'm sure you must have been there till dawn with the other young people."

At thirty-eight, I felt like it had been a while since I'd last been lumped in with the 'young people', but I supposed it was all relative. We walked out of the grocery store together and continued at Flora's pace towards the bus station; the rain had almost tapered off, but not quite. "The field will be muddy tonight," I pointed out.

"Aye, maybe a bit," Flora replied. "But the rain will be gone any minute now, you'll see."

Looking up at the solid bank of grey cloud, I had my doubts, but I supposed that she knew more about the weather on the island than I would. "I hope so."

"You'll see," she repeated, then leaned closer, lowering her voice. "I've seen enough of these shows. No matter what season they've come, the weather seems to smile on them. You'll go again tonight." It was a statement, not a question.

"Definitely."

She nodded. "I'll be going down, but only for a while. At my age, you can only do so many late nights. So, was it what you expected?"

It took me a while to decide how to answer that. "I'm not sure what I expected," I said eventually. "My great-gran only told me what she saw in one of the tents specifically, and I didn't see that last night. But I guess I would say yes and no. It was every bit as amazing as I had thought it would be, and at the same time, whatever I did think I expected didn't really prepare me for what it was really like. The food took me by surprise," I added, as an afterthought. "Do you really think it's just regular food? I can't imagine them… you know, cooking."

"I've wondered that too. It must come from somewhere, I think – I mean, you do feel like you've eaten something, so they must make it somehow. And they've got the whole day. I always found it harder to imagine them in line at the Tesco," she said, with a laugh.

That actually made me look over my shoulder, just in case. I couldn't quite picture the magicians in the grocery store either, but after all, I had encountered one of them in a pub, on the ferry, and in an art gallery. None of those seemed quite so mundane as the late-afternoon express queue, though.

A car drove past, slowed down, and reversed back to us: Flora smiled and waved, and introduced the driver as her son Alec. He got out and opened the door for his mother, and they offered me a lift back as well. It was welcome, especially when we passed by the bus station and saw a large group of people already waiting, nearly half an hour before the bus was due. "Wow, the word must be spreading now," I said, looking out the rear window as we turned onto Kenneth Street.

"There'll be a mob tonight. You sure you won't come?" she said, turning to Alec in the driver's seat.

"Ah, no. Catriona's having all her schoolmates over for a slumber party. Stuck on my own with half a dozen eleven-year-old girls! My wife's in Lochboisdale visiting her dad," he explained to me, half-turning his head. "I'll try and get to the magic show next weekend."

"The girls would love it," Flora countered.

"Aye, I'm sure they would, but chasing them in every direction half the night and keeping them all out of trouble is not my idea of a good Saturday night out. Besides, Cat's just getting old enough now to get her head right turned by all of that. If she was still six or seven, I wouldn't mind, or if she wants to go on her own when she's grown up."

"And you think I should have stopped you going, when you were young?"

"I was sixteen the first time. Eleven's not sixteen, Mum."

They bickered on for a while; I did my best to ignore it and watch the scenery. At each of the scattered bus stops we passed, there were definitely more people than I had seen on my way into town. I was glad I'd found a place to stay in the village before word got out; I had a feeling that there would be no vacancies anywhere in the area that night.

Callanish was still quiet when they dropped me off at a quarter to six, although not quite so quiet as the day before. True to Flora's prediction, the rain had stopped and the clouds had started to thin a little; I could see a solitary ray of light coming down through a tiny patch of open sky, and pulled out my camera to try to capture it. If the break in the clouds was just a little further north, the sunbeam might have even caught the standing stones. I could see the stones from the cottage window as I stopped off for a hasty bite to eat, and even from this distance I could tell there were plenty of people there.

I decided to walk around that way myself, enjoying the feeling of slipping in through the back gate as though I lived there. The site felt less mysterious, but only a little less, now that it was busy. Some people were clearly tourists, there to add a few snaps to the holiday album before getting back on their charter bus; some looked like locals, presumably whiling away the time before the magicians began another evening of performances. And then there were some who fit neither category, and held my attention just a little more. As I walked around, I amused myself trying to guess who these people might be.

A voice came from right behind my ear suddenly, humming a tune I remembered from my childhood. *One of these things is not like the others...*

Hand over my heart in surprise, I whipped around to see Eric. "Jesus. What are you doing here?"

"I think I know what you're doing here," he replied, not answering my question. "Are you playing the 'who here is a magician' game?"

Caught out, I couldn't think of a way to deny it. "Yeah, I guess. You certainly pulled the wool over my eyes."

He made a face. "I had an unfair advantage, though. You didn't know to look. See who else you can pick out of the lineup."

"You're not the only one here right now?"

"I'm not the only one."

I furrowed my brow, thinking. "Not that guy," I said, nodding discreetly toward a twenty-something man with blond dreadlocks and several piercings. "Too obvious. He'll probably be attending tonight, though."

"Right, and yeah, probably. So, who is it, then?"

"You just want me to guess?"

Eric leaned in close to my ear again. "Call it an educated guess. You know more about us than you think."

I puzzled over that statement while I looked around the site. But then someone did catch my eye. A tall middle-aged woman, smart-casual in a jean jacket over a long sundress: nothing unusual, nothing I could put my finger on, but my attention followed her. A gap in the crowd left her alone at the centre stone for a moment, and in that moment, she reached out to lay her palm on the stone surface. "Her."

"That's one. Who else?"

There were more than one? I kept looking, walking slowly along the path. "The guy in the soccer shirt?" I asked, less certain; the man was accompanied by an eleven- or twelve-year-old boy, clearly his son. I hadn't really considered that the magicians might have children with them, but he carried himself differently.

"Well done. I didn't think you'd spot him. One more."

The last one took more time, but after some deliberation I tentatively decided on a young woman in a woolly sweater, with a braid reaching nearly to her waist.

"You see?" Eric said. "It's not so hard."

I was about to say that I wouldn't have had as much luck on a city street, when the woolly sweater girl came up to us. "What time are you going down, Eric?" she asked, giving me a sidelong glance. Her accent sounded Irish.

Eric looked at the sky, rather than his watch. "I'm going to start kind of later tonight. I need to recharge a bit first. Oh, Claire, this is Heather. Heather, this is Claire. If you find a light-blue tent later, you should see Claire's performance."

Claire shook my hand, but raised one eyebrow very high indeed when Eric referred openly to the performance. "It's okay," he added, but she gave me a strange look as she turned to go.

"Are you not supposed to talk about it?" I asked. "To civilians, that is?"

He shrugged. "There's... some of us have different opinions about that. And I have a theory, anyhow."

When several seconds passed without any elaboration on that statement, I let it go. "How did you wind up here, anyhow?" I asked instead. "I mean, not here here. I know you came on the ferry, obviously, and then presumably drove or something." I was on the verge of babbling, nervous now that I was asking a real question. "How did you get to be part of this?"

Eric ran a hand through his hair, leaving it in disarray. "That, Heather, is a long story. Short version is that I sort of inherited it. The long version... I'll have to tell you another time." Out of the corner of my eye I noticed the tall woman move past, toward the back gate; the young boy and his father were close behind. "I should get ready for tonight," he added, glancing around. He patted my shoulder. "I'll see you later, okay?"

I took that as my cue to go. At the gate, I turned for a moment to look back, and saw Eric standing close to one of the massive slabs of gneiss, both his palms against it. I wondered, but left him to his preparations.

CHAPTER TWENTY

The carnival looked the same from a distance, but when I started walking around I realized that things had changed, just a little. Some tents that I had passed by the night before, intending to come back to, had gone; others had moved. The marquee with the groaning tables of food was nowhere to be seen, but there were people walking around here and there with trays of small edibles, rather like cigarette girls in old-fashioned movies.

Many people were heading into the largest pavilion, the menagerie; it was lit the brightest, and was the most visible from the front gate. I passed that one by for now, partly because I had seen it – though I suspected there might be a completely different act there tonight – and partly due to the crowd. People were streaming in the gate now, and if I looked out beyond the field of tents I could see that cars were parked all along the verge of the little single-track road. I hated to think how they were all going to get back out in random order later on.

I passed a group of girls taking selfies against the backdrop of colours and lights. "Thank god it's working now," one of them was saying, as they all peered over her shoulder at her phone. "Did you see when I tried to take a photo inside? It was like the camera didn't work at all."

"And look, you've got no bars," one of her friends pointed out. "There's no reception here; I tried to text Jamie but it wouldn't go through. I wanted to tell him to come down here and give us a lift back later so we don't have to catch the last bus."

"That's rubbish. How can we get a signal at Tolsta and not here?" complained the third girl.

I walked on at that point, but the moment of eavesdropping had given me something else to think about. My own phone had been on airplane mode for most of the trip, apart from using it at wi-fi hotspots to check my email. And although I had taken all sorts of photos in Edinburgh and Stornoway, I had been so overwhelmed the night before that it hadn't even occurred to me to pull it out. But an event like this was exactly the kind of thing that people would want to capture in pictures, text friends about, and put on their social media feeds. Was that even possible?

Pulling out my phone, I switched it to selfie mode and snapped myself at the head of an aisle of small tents; it was captured, though a little blurry. And there had been that one image published in the newspaper in the seventies, after all. But maybe they had ways of stopping people recording what was going on within the marquees. I filed this away with my expanding list of questions to put to Eric when I saw him again.

I was keeping an eye out for the emerald green tent, and also for the light blue one that he had said was Claire's, but in the meantime I visited several others, each seemingly stranger than the last. At a far corner of the field, a little removed from the crowds and noise, I came across the smallest one I had yet seen; it looked like something you would go camping with. Or at least it would have, were it not for the fact that its sides were black – almost invisible in the deepening night, I had nearly walked by it without noticing – and bore a design in an even deeper black, liquid-looking as if it had just been freshly worked over by a calligrapher. I had to bend almost double to get through the low entrance, but was just barely able to stand up inside.

A small woman sat on a large square cushion on the ground, and beckoned for me to do the same. We were the only people inside. Somewhat awkwardly, I took a seat on the round pillow opposite her, our knees nearly touching. I didn't want to stare, but couldn't help myself; she seemed at first glance to be almost impossibly old, but her posture and face were full of energy. If she had sprung up and done cartwheels, it might not have surprised me, even though she could not possibly be a day under ninety. "Give me your hand," she said, low and steady, her voice showing none of the tremor I remembered from my great-grandmother and still heard in my grandmother.

Was it to be palm reading, then? I did as she requested, thinking that after all, this might be the most normal thing I had run into in the whole of this carnival. I should have known better.

The woman turned my hand over and back in her two wizened ones, then touched the long nail of her index finger to the base of my thumb. A ghostly image of a flower rose into the air and faded away almost as quickly. "Heather, is it?" she said, not really asking. As she traced the contours of my hand, a picture of my life arose, literally; the likenesses of people and events from my thirty-eight years on earth danced through the air like a poorly-edited film.

She ran her thumb along my lifeline – the only thing I knew about fortune-telling – and leaned in to peer at it, lifting a small candle holder with her free hand and bringing it close. "Unusual," she murmured, more to herself than to me. "Let us see…"

Putting the candle down, she dropped my right hand and took up my left, bending it back so that the inside of my wrist was exposed. With a word that I didn't recognize as any language I knew, she put two fingers there, as if intending to take my pulse. I felt heat radiating out from the spot, almost to the point of pain; I looked at her in alarm, but only for a second, because then my wrist started to glow. The two small veins that were usually just barely visible there were standing out in stark relief, silver like trickles of mercury disappearing gradually under my flesh.

This, it seemed, had been unexpected for the palm-reader as well, but she covered it quickly. Taking my right hand again, she did the same thing, with the same result. Without comment, she went back to my palm; this time the images were hazier, harder to distinguish. "The future," she said, "is fluid. You are at a crossroads. You will… learn something about yourself, and have to make a choice. I cannot see beyond it."

Back outside in the open air, the night quite clear now, I contemplated the encounter. *You will learn something about yourself.* I had a feeling the old woman already knew what that was, but would not say.

CHAPTER TWENTY-ONE

I was still mulling over the fortune-teller's words – and the look of surprise she'd quickly concealed when she had performed the trick with my veins – when I bumped up against someone's shoulder. "Sorry," I said automatically, registering a woman in what looked like a medieval gown before I saw the face and realized that it was Claire, who I'd met at the standing stones. "Sorry about that," I repeated.

"It's alright; I think I bumped you." She glanced over her shoulder; no one else was within ten feet of us. "Look, I'm sorry if I was a bit short with you earlier; it's not like you're exactly an outsider, yeah? I'm just on my way to start – why don't you come?" She pointed me down a very narrow gap between two tents. "You'll see mine just opposite when you pop out through there. I've got to go round the other way."

Down the narrow passage I went, nearly tripping on a guy rope in the dark, and came out on the other side into one of the busiest lanes of the field. I could have sworn I'd been past this way already, but if so, the pale blue tent had not been there before.

The cold took my breath away for a moment when I stepped in, and the ground crunched with frost under foot. I didn't see any kind of seating; instead, people were standing around, pulling their jackets and sweaters around themselves. A moment after I came in, Claire walked out from behind a silk screen; in her silver gown, she matched the pale colours around her. Lifting both her hands, palms up, above her head, she closed her eyes and took a deep breath. The next thing I knew, snow flurries were falling: they seemed to be emanating from her somehow, though I could not see exactly where. The flakes grew larger, fluffy like a postcard Christmas scene. When the ground was white, she let the snowfall slow, and picked up a glass bottle that looked to be full of water; when tipped in the air, it spilled out but immediately turned to ice, leaving a delicate curved shape floating precariously in mid-air. With a breath, she shattered it, the tiny crystals falling to the ground like broken glass and glittering there in the ambient light. Bowing, she made it clear that the performance was done, at least for now: it had only taken moments, but the effect was stunning. I joined in the cheers as she left the way she had come in.

It was not a hot night, at least by my usual experience of August, but stepping out of the tent I felt the mild air begin to strip away the chill. There was a lengthy queue outside the menagerie now, and another, nearly as long, outside a velvety purple tent of a similar size; I didn't feel like waiting in line, but made a mental note to come back later in the night after some of the crowds had gone. Instead, I found my way to a tent full of fire acts: juggling, swallowing, dancing, all things I had seen done before, but not with this sort of skill. One older man in a traditional tails jacket and top hat struck me as a ringmaster of sorts; he strode tirelessly around the tent, speaking to people and surprising them with tricks. When he came up to me, he tilted his head slightly, seeming to appraise me. "Have we met before, my dear?"

I shook my head. "No." If I had met this man before – even outside, in what I couldn't help thinking of as the real world – I was sure I would have remembered him. His voice was a deep, rich bass, and his face was etched with laugh lines, like a wood carving; when he tipped his hat to me, he was revealed as entirely bald. "I'm Heather," I added, not wanting to sound rude.

"Winston," he replied, giving me a courtly bow. "How do you know this place? Who were your parents?"

The questions took me by surprise, and made me a little uneasy. I backed away without answering and left the tent, taking deep breaths of the damp night air. A young man was passing with one of the trays that was like a cigarette box. "You look like you could use a drink, love," he said, producing a small silver mug with some kind of steaming beverage in it.

I rather agreed with the sentiment. Just as I was taking the cup from his hand, though, an arm reached round and took it from me. "Be careful what you take from this guy."

Eric's sudden appearances were becoming less surprising. "Why?" I asked, looking back and forth between them.

He took a small sip. "Admit it, Luke. How much whisky is in this?"

Looking like a kid caught with his hand in the cookie jar, Luke shrugged. "Well, it's a bit strong. Do you still want one?"

I took a fresh cup and thanked him, but did sip it more delicately than I otherwise might have. It tasted of spices and honey, and I would have barely known there was alcohol in it had I not been warned. "Thanks for the heads-up," I said, falling into step beside Eric as he headed in the opposite direction from Luke. "I was afraid that it might have been drugged or something, though, the way you took it away." With another sip, I could feel my head buzzing just a little; I would have been in a state if I had drunk the whole thing quickly.

Eric shook his head. "No, nothing like that. I've been part of this for twenty-five years now, and I can promise you you're basically safe here."

"Basically?"

"Well, we're all human. I've seen a few fistfights, a few broken hearts. Some people sleep around." He looked back in the direction we'd come. "Luke's a good kid at heart, but he's got some growing up to do. He likes to get drunk with girls and see what ensues."

"Were you different at that age?" I couldn't resist asking.

He had been taking a sip of the hot toddy as I'd said it, and choked a bit as he started to laugh. Coughing, he shook his head. "No, probably not so different, except that I certainly wasn't living like this at nineteen. He was born here, though – I mean, not here, but as part of this."

I did a bit of math in my head; if Eric had been with the magicians for twenty-five years, but not at age nineteen, that meant that he had to be forty-five, at the very least. I'd thought that he was closer to my own age – if not younger - but I was too polite to ask. Instead, I told him about my encounter in the fire tent. "I didn't know what to say," I concluded. "He seemed... intense."

"Winston is intense. But there's a reason he asked you about your family. There's sometimes..." He paused, considering his words. "What I said about the sleeping around – every once in a while, somebody turns up claiming to be the child of somebody here."

"Well, that's certainly not me. The only person in my family who ever saw the magicians was my great-grandmother." I suddenly remembered all the questions he had asked me on the ferry from Ullapool. "That's what you were trying to figure out on the boat, wasn't it? Whether I was one of those people?"

"I guess you've got me there. You're sure nothing happened with your great-grandmother, right?"

We had come around to the back of the field, and were walking along the last aisle; there were not nearly so many visitors here. "I'd wondered, I admit, but she didn't have her first child till three years later. She did have a romance, though, and told me she realized later that she hadn't been the only one who'd fallen for the same guy."

"Was his name Raffaele?"

I stopped in surprise. "Yes. How did you know?"

Eric ran his hand through his hair. "He's a bit... notorious. There's quite a few people here who are descended from him in some way or other. He was still trying to seduce women well into his old age; I always thought he was a conceited jackass, but up until pretty recently we'd still get ladies asking to see him."

"You met him?" Again, I was trying to do math. "How recently?"

"Ummm... well, he lived to a really old age." He looked around. "Look, Heather, there's a lot you don't know about us. I can't really lay it all out right now; I've got to go on soon. What are you doing tomorrow?"

"Do you guys still not perform on Sundays?"

He shook his head. "Not here. If we don't respect the traditions of the place, we wear out our welcome a lot more quickly. You're staying at the Kestrel Cottage, right?"

"Okay, now I know I didn't tell you that. Do you read minds, as well?"

"It's barely even a village, Heather. There's only about three places anybody can stay. Besides, Flora Nicolson told me. Anyhow, if you're still here in a couple of hours, you should come by the big purple tent. There'll be a bit of a ceilidh – you know, a party - once the crowd clears out a bit. You should join us."

CHAPTER TWENTY-TWO

I went to Eric's performance next, wondering whether it would be similar to the night before. The first difference that I couldn't help noticing was that there were easily twice the number of people in the audience; I had to stand, squeezing into a spot behind one of the benches.

He held everyone spellbound once again, this time shaping the mists into a series of mythical beasts: centaurs, griffins, and a dragon that appeared so solid it made half the spectators flinch as it circled the room. Afterwards, I wandered the show on my own, hoping to press him for more information, but he was nowhere to be found. There was nothing for it but to follow his suggestion and slowly make my way back towards the purple velvet tent.

By this time it was nearly one in the morning; the crowd had started to thin around midnight, and it seemed like most people were heading toward the gate and out to their cars, as the lights and colours began to go dark. I saw no lineup outside the tent, but when I approached the entrance, a woman stepped out to bar the way. "Show's all done for tonight, love."

"Eric said I should come," I countered, feeling more than a little unsure of myself. "For the ceilidh."

Her countenance changed. "That's the magic word," she said,

smiling. "Do come in."

I had no idea what the tent normally looked like on the inside, but now it was almost wall-to-wall people, and I was certain that the majority of them were magicians. Some faces I recognized, and others were casually reeling off little illusions – not for show, but seemingly for practice, or even just as a sort of half-conscious tic, like the man idly flicking blue sparks off the tips of his fingers as he talked to a group of people. There was a woman with disturbingly natural-looking cat ears and tail, and several of them were still in their stage attire, giving the whole thing an air of a fancy-dress party.

Music was playing; I couldn't see where it was coming from at first, but eventually I wove my way towards one end and saw a group of people, chairs drawn up into a circle, playing instruments: a hand drum, a couple of guitars, a fiddle and a flute. A lanky man strolled over with a trumpet and joined in, improvising his way into the tune.

Someone passed a glass into my hand. Thinking of the deceptive whisky drink earlier, I was careful to sip it slowly as I found a spot to perch on the edge of a raised platform, where I could see the musicians and the people who were beginning to dance. A guitar was passed to someone else, a fiddler sat out and an accordion materialized from somewhere; it was all very loose by comparison to the elegant performances, and I realized that I had been privileged to be invited as the magicians let their hair down on a Saturday night.

"Are you dancing?" It was Luke, the purveyor of the whisky, and without waiting for an answer he took me by both hands and pulled me onto the ersatz dance floor. It was some kind of traditional dance, a reel maybe; I had no idea what I was doing but found it not too hard to follow as I was swung around from partner to partner and back to Luke again. "I knew you shouldn't be sitting on the sidelines," he said, as we went around each other in circles, first with right palms together, then left. "You're good."

"And you're half my age," I pointed out.

He laughed. "I like a challenge."

The partners changed again then, and I could see him launching into his flattery on the next woman. I was whisked through three more rounds of the dance before I finally begged off, needing a chance to catch my breath. As I left the dancers behind, I glimpsed Eric across the tent, but I didn't have the energy to fight my way through the crowd; I was sure I'd talk to him eventually. Instead, I found Claire coming to sit next to me on a bench at the side.

"You found us," she said.

I nodded. "You do know how to throw a party. I don't mean to intrude, though."

"Nonsense." She waved a hand. "It's open to anyone who knows it's going on. Eric said this is your first time; do you have a family connection here?"

I wondered for a moment whether she meant the location, or the people within the pavilion. "Yes and no. My great-grandmother came from here, and told me about you – not you personally, you know what I mean – and she had some kind of a fling with a man named Raffaele." I saw the flicker of recognition at the name. "But I'm not his long-lost great-grandchild or anything. My gran was born three years too late for that."

Claire pursed her lips a little, looking at my face. "You're sure, then?"

"Trust me, I've done the math." I laughed a little. "When I was thirteen and first heard about all this, I did like to imagine that it might have been true, though. At that point it had never occurred to me that you guys would ever come back, either."

A smile played about the corners of her mouth. "When I was thirteen I used to try to imagine what it would be like to be a regular girl, and go out to school."

So she was another one who'd been born into this. "You were

home-schooled, I guess?"

"In a manner of speaking. There's a few of us around the same age, so we had a school of sorts. I guess we learned enough, since I sat my exams and got into uni."

"What did you study?"

"Anthropology." She reached her hands behind her head, deftly arranging her long hair back into a braid. "I guess I wanted to understand the strange little tribe I come from, yeah?"

"Me too. I mean, I did Anthropology as well," I said. Strange that we should find such a normal common ground in this context. "And then… did you come right back to this afterwards?"

Claire sighed. "I experimented with being a normal person for a couple of years. If nothing else, I did fall in love with Dublin. The so-called homeland, even though I'm the umpteenth generation of… this. Took a job slinging pints, messed about with some nice, regular boys. Polished up my accent," she added, with a laugh. "I go back there in between, when we're not travelling. But this is home."

She pointed out her parents to me: a red-haired lady and a handsome blond man near the centre of the dance floor. There was quite an age gap, I thought – her father looked to be sixty or so, while her mother seemed barely old enough to actually be her mother – but they looked extremely happy. "My grandparents retired, in a manner of speaking, a couple years ago. They only come with us once or twice a year now."

"Do you have any brothers or sisters?" I asked, unable to help my curiosity about what it would be like to grow up like this.

"Ah… I grew up an only child," she said, though there was a pause there. Changing the topic, she began to ask me more about my life. Public school, having a younger sister, childhood in Canada, all of this was apparently fascinating; I began to wonder who was the stranger specimen, her or me.

It was on the dance floor that I ran into Eric again – almost literally, as I fumbled a step and practically collided with him. "Sorry," I told him. "I was doing better at this a drink or two ago."

He laughed. "It's okay, I've done far worse." We both spun away to other partners, and by the time the song came to a close I had lost track of him once more.

Despite my best efforts, I ran out of energy before the festivities showed signs of winding down. It was twenty past three when I slowly made my way up the road to the cottage. Once away from the tents, the landscape was incredibly dark, particularly this late at night. No moon was visible, but the sky, almost cloudless now, was alive with stars; living in a big city, the last time I had seen so many had been in a massive power failure ten years before. I thought I saw movement, a shooting star, but I didn't know what more I could wish for.

CHAPTER TWENTY-THREE

I slept late again, but it was Sunday; there was nowhere to hurry to, and no way to get there if there was. Turning on the radio, I listened for the weather forecast: windy – no surprise there – with increasing cloud, rain likely in the late afternoon and evening. If I was going to go out, now seemed the time to do it. After breakfast, I pulled on a sweater and went walking.

Towards the standing stones first: from the gate, I could recognize many faces among those moving about the stones, but not Eric or Claire. I did see Winston, and when he looked my way I decided to continue on my walk rather than risk another uncomfortable interrogation.

Instead, I took a circle down by the lower road, past the farm and the field of tents, quiet now, and back up round a bend to a crossroads. Left would take me back to the cottage; I went right, where the road narrowed yet further. A loose border collie startled me with a bark, but then tagged along good-naturedly for a hundred metres or so before returning to its home. Other than that, I saw few signs of life till I came to where the road ended, at a small graveyard looking over the water towards the next village. A woman perhaps a little over my mum's age was pushing a man in a wheelchair, presumably just coming from the cemetery.

She nodded, and I bid her good morning. The man in the chair squinted up at me, but said nothing. He looked incredibly elderly, even more so than the fortune teller I had encountered the night before. His sparse white hair hung down to his shoulders, and a thick blanket rested on his lap. Although the weather was pleasant, I was surprised that they were out walking and not taking a car.

I did not enter the graveyard. However, the area round it was quite beautiful, so I walked round the boundary fence and took a number of photos, before slowly making my way back. Halfway along the road, I glanced at Flora's house and saw her wave from the window. Perhaps it was as good a time as any to take her up on her offer of tea.

She ushered me into a kitchen that was spotless and bright, and looked like it probably had not been changed much in my lifetime, apart from a microwave of fairly recent vintage. Something about it put me in mind of summer breakfasts at Granny Chrissie's, and I felt very much at ease – that is, until I was surprised to see Claire in the doorway, followed by her parents. "Fancy meeting you here," she said.

Flora laughed at the expression on my face. "They're staying here, love, along with a few others. Colleen and Ben have my spare room," she said, nodding to indicate Claire's mother and father, "and some of the other young folk are staying in the old barn. My son – Alec, you met him - made it over into a sort of bunkhouse years ago; he had great plans to start a youth hostel but it fizzled out when he got married. Works just nicely at times like this, though."

"I had wondered where everyone slept, I admit," I told them, glancing out the back window. A couple of young were sitting on a bench outside a low stone building that looked a good bit older than the one we were in; perhaps it had been the original house before becoming first a barn and now a dormitory. "Nice as the tents are, I couldn't imagine all of you camping out."

Colleen shook her head. "We're lucky to have… friends, most everywhere we go, who manage to put us up with barely a moment's notice."

"Not all here, though," Claire added, taking the kettle off the stove and filling a large brown teapot. "We're scattered around. Some people are staying at An Drochaid - we know the family that own the land – and a few other places."

"I remember when we still used to travel in caravans." Ben refused the last available chair, leaning against the doorframe instead. "Real ones, mind you: the horse-drawn sort. We'd sleep in the caravans, then."

"That must have been when you were very young," I blurted out, without thinking.

He smiled. "Oh, not as young as you might think, darling."

"Mr… Ben," I amended, wanting to be polite but realizing I had no clue what his last name might be. "When you were young, you would have known a man named Raffaele, right?"

"I still do know him."

I shook my head. "No, I mean… I don't know exactly how old, but he was an adult when my great-grandmother met him in nineteen-twenty. I heard he lived to an old age, so I assumed you must have known him at some point."

Colleen shot him a look, but he disregarded it. "No, I know who you're talking about. He's well up in years, but he's still this side of the grave. Only just."

One hundred and eleven. If he had been the same age as Granny Chrissie – and in my mind's eye, I had always pictured him slightly older – and was somehow still alive, he would have to be 111 years old. It was within the realm of possibility, but shocking all the same. "Is he still…" I was about to correct myself; it was ridiculous to think he might still be among the magicians here. Or was it? "Was that him I just saw, in a wheelchair, down by the graveyard? Hair down to his shoulders? He was with a grey-haired lady in a red coat."

Ben sighed. "Had to be. He's ill now, and this is probably his last trip that isn't in a pine box, and he knows it. But he was determined to come here one more time."

This changed everything. "Could I see him? Is he still... I mean, mentally, does he still have his faculties?"

"Oh yes, his memory's still sharp," Ben said, but at this point his wife cut him off.

"I understand you'll want to see him," she said, leaning across the table, her brow furrowed. "Just don't... I'm sure your great-granny remembered him fondly in her later years, but don't cherish too many romantic ideas about him."

I nodded, thinking of how Eric had described him. "Even my great-gran told me that he'd had a girl in every port, or more than one, as she put it. And then I've heard he had... rather a lot of offspring."

"Who told you that?"

"It was..." Out of the corner of my eye, I saw Claire shake her head surreptitiously, while her mother wasn't looking. "Luke," I lied, substituting the first alternate name that came to mind, and wondering why she didn't seem to want me to mention Eric. "He said something about it."

Colleen nodded, and I could see Claire give a sigh of relief. "He would. His granddad is one of Raffaele's bastards, probably the favourite of the litter. Thank god for birth control, for Luke's going down the same road if somebody doesn't smarten him up. Sorry," she added. "That was coarse, but I don't think living like we do is an excuse to be promiscuous."

"Of course not." Flora spoke for the first time since welcoming me into the kitchen, as she set a plate of scones on the table. "Ben, maybe you could take Heather to see Raffaele tomorrow? If he's been out and about today, no doubt he'll be too tired this afternoon."

And so it was arranged. Even though we spent an hour over tea, talking about other things, Raffaele was still foremost in my mind when I eventually took my leave. Turning into the lane of the cottage, I was busy debating what exactly I wanted to say to him, and didn't notice Eric sitting on the front step till I was almost at the door.

"Have you been waiting here long? I'm sorry." He had suggested that we talk, but I didn't remember either of us making a specific plan of it. "I was at Flora's."

He stood up, waving it off. "It's a nice day. I don't mind. Do you want to go for a walk?"

I had already been walking, but he was right: it was still a pleasant day, and what else would we have done? "Sure."

On the way, I recounted my morning's experience. "I'm sorry I didn't tell you he was still alive," Eric said, looking into the wind for a moment. "I thought it might be a bit much to process, and I didn't want to drop that bombshell on you and run."

"How old is he, anyways? Do you know?"

He shook his head. "I don't know. Old. Freaky old. But…"

"But?"

"They say this… life, it keeps you young. Maybe that kept him going."

We continued on, past the standing stones and out toward the main road; Eric pointed us to the right, and after a few minutes we turned down a path that I remembered from years before as leading to one of the smaller stone circles. On the way, I mused aloud about some of the questions I wanted to ask Raffaele, trying to prioritize them since I was sure that – magic keeping one young or not – a man of his incredible age wouldn't have the energy for a long conversation.

That train of thought petered out around the time we reached the fence that surrounded the circle, and I remembered a smaller detail from my visit to Flora's. "When I was talking to Claire's parents about this, it came up about him having knocked up a lot of girls in his younger days... Thanks," I added, as Eric gave me his hand to help me over the rickety stile. "And... they were asking how I knew about it, and I caught Claire giving me a kill signal when I was about to mention your name. Maybe I misinterpreted, but..."

"No, you didn't." He hopped easily over the fence, then sat down on the stile. "It's a bit touchy. You know I haven't done this my whole life, right?"

"Right. You said you were from Buffalo, and you've been with the magicians... what, twenty-five years?"

"Do you know how I came to join them?"

No one had told me anything about that, but I had certainly wondered, and said so. Eric nodded. "I wasn't sure if Claire might have said something, but I'd better start at the beginning. I think I told you that most of my family never left the US?"

"You said you were the black sheep."

He raised his eyebrows. "Well, yeah. But my parents were too, before me. I was born at Ramstein Air Base, in Germany. They met there; my mom was a nurse on the base, and my dad was Air Force. When I was about five or so, my dad was sent to Viet Nam, so my mom and I went back to the States and moved in with my grandparents..."

"Wait a second," I interrupted. My grasp of American history was an outline at best, but I was pretty sure that the Viet Nam war had ended around the time that I was born. "You were already five when Viet Nam was still going on?"

"I guess it was history by the time you came along," he said. "For the record, I was born in nineteen-sixty."

"You're fifty-three?" I exclaimed, then immediately felt embarrassed. "I mean... wow. Apparently this really does keep you young."

"Oh, come here." He stood up to give me a half-hug. "Thanks. Anyhow, I'm not going to bore you with my whole life story; the nutshell version is that my dad came back, we settled into a nice all-American life, younger brother and sister came along, very happy, et cetera. It wasn't till I turned twenty-one that I found out that there was more to the story. My mom and dad took me out for a birthday dinner, just the three of us, and after the excitement of my first legal beer, they told me that I was, for all intents and purposes, adopted."

"That must have been a shock."

"I'll say. Technically, I'm half-adopted, although there's no paperwork that says so. Turns out my mom was already pregnant when she met my dad; he fell in love with her anyways, and they figured it was best to keep the truth to themselves."

I began to see where this might be going. "And... some time in nineteen-fifty-nine or so, your mother visited a mysterious group of magicians, somewhere near the military base?" When he nodded, I asked the obvious question. "Is Raffaele your father?"

Eric shook his head. "No. He'd moved on to slightly older women by that time, I guess; the last of his kids that I know about is about ten or twelve years older than me. But let me backtrack a bit. I didn't get the whole story – the circumstances, and especially the name – out of my mom till a couple of years later. I think she knew I'd want to go track them – him – down. She told me about seeing the magicians in a little village, just before Christmas, and falling in love with one of them. Apparently he asked her to go with him, even offered to leave the magicians and stay with her. She was too straight-laced to 'take up with a bunch of gypsies', as she put it – although apparently not too straight-laced to sleep with one of them – and she said she was afraid to ask him to leave his family in case he hated her for it later. By the time she realized that I was on the way, they were long gone."

"And then she met your dad."

"And you know, they've had a happy life. She says he's the

one she was meant to be with, and I believe it."

"Sounds like my great-gran," I said. "But I know how badly I wanted to find... all of this. I can imagine it would be even more so, knowing your... well, your biological father was out here."

"Exactly." Eric was pacing back and forth now. "It took me four years to find them the first time; they were in the same village where my mom had seen them, but I just missed them as they were leaving town. The next summer, I managed a bit of lucky guesswork, and caught them at Avignon. I met my father – who obviously had never known I existed - and he said I'd inherited his talent, asked me to stay."

"And you did."

"Not at first. I never thought I was coming to run away with them. He kept giving me the card, telling me where they'd be next, until later that fall I gave in to the inevitable. The only complication was, that he'd gone on with his life as well; he was married, with a baby daughter, so it was a bit weird that he had this twenty-eight-year-old son showing up. Not that I was looking for him to be a father – I've already got one – but still... I can imagine his wife didn't appreciate finding out that he'd once been ready to give it all up for my mom."

I waited for more information, but he offered none. After about a minute, I tentatively put the pieces together. "And that baby daughter was.... Claire?" I remembered that pause in her answer, when I'd asked her about siblings. When Eric nodded, I went on. "Which mathematically has to mean that Ben is a fair bit older than he looks, too, unless he was about thirteen when he met your mom. This is all very complicated."

Eric shrugged. "We're humans, Heather. Get a hundred or so people living together, travelling together, working together in really close quarters, living out of suitcases and backpacks for big parts of the year, and a certain amount of drama is bound to happen. Especially given some of the things some of us are capable of," he added, with a laugh. "Colleen's never quite warmed to me;

it's not the end of the world. I've got my real family back in the States, and then this crowd here – not just Ben and Claire, specifically, but the whole gang – and this is kind of a real family too."

CHAPTER TWENTY-FOUR

On Monday afternoon, Colleen came and knocked at the door to tell me that it was time to go and see Raffaele. "He doesn't often have patience for meeting new people these days, so don't take it personally if he's not got much to say to you," she warned, as we walked around to the farm. "Twenty years ago, he still would have tried to flirt and be charming, but he hasn't the energy now. Ben says he's a ghost already, that's just forgotten to die."

We were met at the door by the woman I'd seen pushing the wheelchair the day before; I was getting used to the fact that most of the magicians looked entirely ordinary when taken out of context. Colleen introduced her as Isabella, but Isabella didn't seem very much interested in making my acquaintance. She led me into a small room off the kitchen that had been made into a sort of a bedroom; a window looked out onto the field of tents and on a narrow bed, propped up with pillows, the frail form of Raffaele sat gazing out.

"The girl is here, Papa," Isabella said, fluffing up an extra cushion and placing it behind the invalid's head. "She says you knew her grandmother."

I cleared my throat nervously. "Great-grandmother."

Raffaele turned at that, and I saw him properly for the first time. His feet reached nearly to the end of the bed even in a half-sitting position; the passing of time had apparently not shrunken him much vertically, but he was terribly thin and gaunt, his olive skin wrinkled and ashen, marred with age spots. It stretched the limits of my imagination to try and picture him the way Granny Chrissie had described – so handsome once, that he had rendered her dizzy and breathless. He was dying; that much was clear.

"Come here, child," he said, his voice not so creaky as I would have expected. He had an Italian accent, but only a slight one. When I came closer, he appraised me for a minute or two, then sent Isabella from the room. "I know your face," he said, when we were alone. "You have her eyes. Chrissie Morrison." He closed his eyes a moment, as if picturing her as she had been, ninety-three years before. "She was your…"

"Great-grandmother," I repeated. "She told me about you, years ago. She…" I tried to think how to put it. "She remembered you fondly."

"Remembered," he echoed. "She is gone, then?"

"Seventeen years ago. And she was ninety-four," I couldn't help adding. "I hope it's not rude to say this, sir, but I was shocked to find out that you're still alive."

He sighed, ignoring my comment. "They are all gone, you know. All the women I loved."

"You loved her?" I refrained from stating the rest of my thought – that he had not left her with that impression.

"I did. In my way. I never looked for a wife." He went silent for long enough that I was about to ask him another question, then he continued when I least expected it. "Chrissie, she was the most delicate flower, so tiny and perfect, and so sad. She was lovely, and I was not allowed to have her, so I loved her all the more."

"What do you mean, not allowed to have her?"

"Well, she was Sébastien's child, of course," he replied, as if I were extremely dense to have asked. "He knew her at once, when first he saw her step out from my tent, though he had never laid eyes on her before. Sébastien had always said that he would know any bastard of his on sight, though I could not tell you how. She did not resemble him greatly."

"She wasn't a bastard!" I blurted out in astonishment.

Raffaele gave a dry, raspy laugh. "You do not question that your great-grandmother knew romance as a young girl, and yet you cannot imagine that your great-grandmother's mother had known the same?" He shook his head, and looked back out the window again, but kept talking. "Sébastien was the best of us. He had only just plucked me out of the Circo Torinese when we came here and he met a lady, married with many sons, poor, but still beautiful in her way. He said he could seduce any woman, and he did so. Nineteen years later, we return, and find that she bore him a daughter, though we never saw the lady nor any other of her family again. That daughter was called Chrissie, though Sébastien insisted on calling her Christiane."

"She never told me this."

Raffaele shook his head. "She never knew. What purpose would it have served? He was just interested enough in her welfare that he forbade me to know her in the way that I would have wished, but he never wanted to gather family to his side, and there must have been more of them by then; he was already seventy when he met Chrissie's mother."

I shuddered a little, but then again, based on my experience with the magicians so far, he had probably been seventy and looked forty-five. "My great-gran – Chrissie – said that she wasn't the only girl you romanced while you were here, though."

There was that laugh again. "I could not have her, but there were so many young girls, all waiting for a man's attention. There were so few young men in those days, you see. It was all too easy." The laugh turned into a fit of coughing this time, and it did not abate; I stood up in some alarm, wondering if there was anything I could do, but Isabella came in and tended to him.

"You should go," she said, not looking at me, but then Raffaele managed to say something to her between spasms. "He says to come back again tomorrow."

That night, I searched through the tents looking for Eric, wanting to talk over this strange news with him, but instead I bumped into Luke. "No dancing tonight, and no drinks," I said pre-emptively, though it didn't look like either was on offer; he was juggling a series of glowing crystal spheres.

"Oh, come on," he said, putting one arm round my waist and continuing to juggle around me. "What's on your mind? You look distracted."

"Raffaele is your great-grandfather, isn't he? I met him today."

"What made him do that? He hasn't seen anyone except Isabella in ages," he asked.

"I wanted to talk to him about my great-grandmother," I said. "She knew him, and he remembered her. Said that he loved her, but… he was warned off her, because she was the daughter of someone… Sebastian?"

"Sébastien," he corrected, looking like he was viewing me in a new light. "That would explain it."

"Explain what?"

He pursed his lips. "Eric didn't tell you? When you grow up here, or spend enough time doing this, you kind of see it on people. You weren't anybody's kid, that was clear, but there's something. If Sébastien was your however-many-greats-grandfather, that would explain it. You're one of us." Deftly catching all the balls in one hand, he removed his other hand from my hip. "I've got to run. Catch you in the silver tent, if you're over that side."

I was one of them. Somehow, it didn't seem as simple as that. I was going to have to ask Raffaele more questions.

CHAPTER TWENTY-FIVE

I made my own way back the next day, and found Isabella expecting me, if no friendlier than the day before. "Papa, the girl is here again," she announced, opening the door and adjusting his blankets a little.

"Good." His voice sounded a little hoarser today. "What is your name, child?"

"Heather. Heather Ross."

"Ross?" He narrowed his eyes at me. "How interesting. From here, then."

I shook my head. "From Glasgow."

"Ah." He lifted his hand, just a little, as if to wave it away. "I just thought... Chrissie had a friend. They came here together, the first time. And... when I was warned away from the one I wanted, I found the friend was nearly as pretty, and quite willing..." He shook his head. "I'm sure her name was Ross."

I thought back to Granny Chrissie's version of their story; as far as I had remembered, she had gone alone to the magicians. Except for the first time... her friend from school, who she roomed with in Stornoway. "And do you remember Miss Ross's first name?"

Raffaele shook his head. "I should be ashamed to admit it, perhaps, but I do not. But I can picture her, though – is that strange? I only remember because Chrissie and she were such a contrast, the one time I saw them together. The one so tiny it seemed that the wind would take her away, and the other tall and hearty. A jolly farm girl that one takes for a tumble behind the stables. You are too modern to be shocked, I see. What a shame."

I wasn't shocked – it fit his character portrait as it had been drawn for me – but I felt a certain belated indignation on Granny Chrissie's behalf, that he should have been romancing her one moment and then knowingly having his way with her friend the next. I was glad now that my great-grandmother hadn't run away with this man.

Not sure how much more I wanted to hear about his escapades, I said my goodbye and stood up to go. But at the door, I realized that there was one thing I absolutely had to ask; I turned back to face him.

"How old are you, really?"

He did not answer straight away, but his face took on a shrewd expression as he looked me up and down.

"I was born on the twenty-first of April. The year was eighteen-seventy-five. Good day, child."

CHAPTER TWENTY-SIX

I realized as I left the farmhouse that I had not the faintest idea where Eric was staying; I would have liked his help to put all of this together. After walking round the village, glancing hopefully at each house as if it might have answers, I decided that I was going to have to assemble some of this puzzle myself. I already had my wallet and bag with me; when I happened to see the bus coming down the road, I flagged it down and rode into Stornoway.

The library had not changed much from my last visit, except for a great deal more computers. "I was wondering if you could help me with some research," I asked the librarian.

"Certainly. Are you looking up your family history?"

That was more or less what I was up to, I supposed. "My great-grandmother was born in Leurbost, and I'm trying to learn more about her childhood. Do you have any… any archival stuff about local schools, or anything like that?" What I really wanted was to find out who the mysterious Miss Ross had been; she bothered me.

"Actually, you're in luck. If you go over to the Museum nan Eilean…" She pulled a town map from behind the desk and drew a route on it. "It's only about a five-minute walk. They've moved out their main exhibits as they'll be moving into a new building, but they've an exhibition on about the island schools; some of our photos and things went on loan there. Your great-grandmother would have gone to the old Leurbost school, and that's one of the ones featured in the exhibit."

It seemed that things were going my way. I followed the directions she had given me and found the museum building on Francis Street, with a prominent sign outside about their impending move. A smaller notice on the door advertised the temporary exhibit 'Our Old School Days'. I pushed open the door, dropped a few coins in the donation box, and went in to have a look around.

As the librarian had said, there was a section of the display that focused on the Leurbost school. A glass case held an attendance sheet – sadly from 1934, too late to be of use to me – and a few textbooks, but most of the exhibition was comprised of photographs. I skimmed over them until a face caught my eye. Yes, I was right: the caption read *Pupils of Leurbost School, 1915*. The slight girl at the end of the row was clearly the younger version of the woman photographed eight years later at the Stornoway pier, the photo that sat framed by my desk back home. Granny Chrissie at thirteen, the same age I had been when I had first learned of her history with the magicians.

She wore a dark, shapeless sort of dress, too big for her, but looked straight at the camera, wearing the amused expression that had caught my attention. Her arm was linked through that of the girl next to her. The other girl's dress was slightly too short - not surprising, as she had a good five inches over tiny Chrissie – and one of her socks was slouched halfway down to her ankle. Her hair was an unruly mass of dark waves that looked to be escaping from some kind of attempt at tying it back. She was smiling more openly than Chrissie; I could imagine the two girls sharing some joke in a whisper while the photographer tried to marshal the students to stay still.

Hanging by the side of the display were a series of laminated sheets that offered more information about the pictures. About this one, it said:

> Photo of Leurbost School pupils, 1915, donated by Mr. Angus Murray of Leurbost. Mr. Murray's grandfather, Domhnall Murray, attended the school and is pictured second from left. Left to right: Malcolm MacNeil, Domhnall Murray, Jessie Campbell, Robina Murray, Peter Mackay, Janet MacNeil, Alec MacLeod, Jean MacNeil, Lizzie MacPhail, Billy Gunn, Ina Ross, Chrissie Morrison.

Seeing my own last name in the list was what I had really been looking for. Ina Ross. Granny Chrissie's best pal; sometime not too long after this photo, they would be gone from school, living together in Stornoway, working full time. Five years after this photo, they would go to see the magicians: Chrissie would have a whirlwind romance and Ina – for there was no doubt she was the Miss Ross remembered by Raffaele – would have a 'tumble behind the stables'. Studying her face again, I searched back in my own memory, trying to think of anything else that Granny Chrissie had said about this girl.

And then it struck me. Chrissie and Ina had fallen out over the magicians, stopped speaking to each other. The last Chrissie had heard of her was of a sudden departure from the island – a departure to Glasgow.

I had a sinking feeling in my stomach. Being single and pregnant in the nineteen-twenties would have been a reason for a young woman to be sent away to the anonymity of a big city, wouldn't it? Ross was a common enough name, of course; there had to have been thousands of Rosses in Glasgow.

But my great-grandmother – my other one, my dad's father's mother, the single mother who had brought up a son on her own – had had an unusual name. It had stuck in my mind because it sounded so ungainly. Murdina Ross. No wonder she had gone by Ina.

It seemed that I was descended from Raffaele after all.

CHAPTER TWENTY-SEVEN

When I entered the magicians' field that evening, I did so with mixed feelings. Did my bloodline actually make me a part of all this, as Luke had claimed? On the contrary: I felt more removed from it than ever. I was walking around half in a daze, not going into any of the tents, when I collided with someone. I apologized automatically, and was about to move on when a hand closed on my arm.

"Hey, Heather, wait a second." It was Eric, dressed for his performance, all in black. "What's wrong?"

I shook my head. "It's nothing. I shouldn't keep you; you must be about to go on."

"Heather, it's after midnight. I was done an hour ago. I... not to sound like a jackass, but I was kind of surprised not to see you. Come on, take a walk with me. I could use some air."

I had wanted so much to talk to him earlier in the day, but now I wasn't even sure which preposterous discovery to begin with; instead, I walked along in silence as he steered us away from the tents, further back into the field, the ground slightly damp underfoot. "Where are we going?"

"Shortcut." He put a hand on my back to guide me round a

hole in the ground. "This way."

We came through the back of another field and up the lane of a house, coming out onto the road a little way down from Kestrel Cottage, towards the stones. He took us that way. Going in through the back gate, I wasn't surprised to find the site completely deserted, the stones only slightly paler than the darkness around them.

Turning his back to me for a moment, he laid a hand on the nearest stone; after a few seconds, he gave the sort of gasp that accompanies the first sip of ice water in a heat wave. "Touch the stones," he said. "You'll feel better."

It was far from being the most improbable thing I'd heard that day, so I tried it. Although not the largest of the stones in the monument, it was still at least twice my height and probably three feet wide; there were plenty of places I could put my hands. I sampled the texture of the rock, skimming my palms over it until I found a smoother spot, one that felt comfortable. And oddly, I discovered that he was right.

"It's peaceful here," I said, not taking my hands away. "Thanks. I think I needed that."

Eric turned, so that he was very gently leaning against the megalith. "So, what's on your mind?"

I debated where to start. "Do all of you come to this because of family connections? I mean, is it genetic?"

It was hard to tell his expression in the darkness. "Not all. It's learned. It's a skill, I think, not so different from any other, except that there aren't many people who can teach it. It's manipulation of energy. I don't know, but I assume probably anyone could learn it, with long enough practice and if they wanted it enough, and if anyone would take them on – but it might take, oh, eighty years or something if you didn't have the gift. The people who have a natural talent for it, it seems like that's usually – not always, but usually – something that runs in families." He paused for a while.

"So, who is it? Who are you related to?"

"A couple of womanizing scumbags, apparently." I had meant to say it with a bit of humour, but it came out more harshly than I expected.

"Wait, what?" He moved a little closer – just as well, since all but his face was practically invisible. "You said there was no way that Raffaele was your great-grandfather."

"Apparently, there was another way," I replied, and explained about Ina Ross. "I was mad, on my Granny Chrissie's behalf, when I first heard the story, but I suppose Ina was my great-gran too. The more I think about it... I never knew much about that branch of the family since my grandfather – Ina's son – died when my dad was just a kid. She never married. I don't think they had a very good life, from what little I know of what kind of man my grandfather was."

"It couldn't have been easy to be a single mom in those days. Maybe it says something, though, that she kept the baby. Wouldn't most women in that situation give it up back then?"

"But he ruined her life!" I protested.

"I guess you can't know for sure, since you can't ask her. I think most mothers wouldn't regret having their child."

Realizing that he must be thinking of his own mother – who had certainly wound up in better circumstances than Ina Ross – I softened my tone. "But their lives must have been so hard; poor and probably not many friends, and he was just... gone. Didn't care what he was leaving behind. And she's dead, and her son is dead, and my Granny Chrissie is dead, and he's still here. How the hell is he still here, when he's..." I had to think about it for a second. "A hundred and thirty-eight years old!" I stepped away from the stone and kicked at the ground; it was an attempt to vent my feelings, but all I managed to do was hurt my foot. Cursing, I sat down on the damp grass.

Eric sat down with me, his back still resting against the stone.

"You said 'a couple'. What else did you find out?"

"That's the thing. The only reason Raffaele even went after Ina was because he was warned off my great-gran – Chrissie, I mean. It's like something out of a goddamn soap opera. And he was warned off of Chrissie because, as it turns out, she was a magician's bastard too. His mentor's, or something."

I heard an intake of breath. "Not Sébastien? Are you serious?"

"That's the one. Seduced a married woman in this case. I suppose that explains why my Granny Chrissie was a surprise baby, and the only girl. Scumbag."

"But that's amazing," Eric replied. "I mean, not that he… Okay, you're right in a lot of ways to say that he was a scumbag – probably worse than you think, actually."

"Thanks. That makes me feel so much better."

"Let me finish. Right, so… I never met Sébastien. He died sometime in the thirties – shot by a jealous husband, in fact, in case that makes you feel any better – but people still talk about him. They say he came out of nowhere, one of those exceptions where somebody with no family connections is born with the gift, and was the best magician anyone had ever seen. Even when they weren't performing, he could… do things. They say he could read minds – not sure how much – and he could make people do things, that he could just talk to someone and they'd want to do what he wanted them to do. Real-life Jedi mind tricks, it sounded like."

"No wonder he said he could seduce any woman."

"Yeah. Kind of makes it hard to say whether it's really consent, doesn't it?" he replied. "Like I said, probably worse than what you already thought. But there's no denying that he was an incredible talent. Maybe you have his genes."

I wasn't sure I wanted them, but there wasn't much I could do about that. Then I remembered the fortune teller; I somehow hadn't had a chance to tell Eric about that either. "Would that be what it meant, then, if the veins in my arms went silver when… I don't know her name, the fortune teller lady, touched them?"

"Sofia. Her name's Sofia. I'm surprised you even found her." He picked up my right hand with his left and pressed his index finger to my wrist; nothing happened. "She did that to me, when I first came. I don't know if it's bloodlines she's seeing, or if it's something else." Apparently realizing that he was still holding my hand, he let it go.

"What else could it be?" I asked.

"Whether or not you have the gift, maybe. I really don't know. Sofia hardly ever shows herself. The older folks here call her the oracle; I think she might be even older than Raffaele." He went silent for a while. "You know, there's a lot of people here descended from Raffaele, but... I don't know if I've ever heard of anyone descended from Sébastien. I don't know why; from everything I've heard, he must have had dozens of kids."

It felt strange to be the one with an answer this time. "Raffaele said that he never... how did he put it? He didn't want to gather children close to him, he had no use for a family. He said that Sébastien knew how to recognize his bastards – it's how he knew Chrissie was one, the first time he saw her – but never let them in on the secret. I don't know how many others there might have been. You'd think that at least some of their mothers would have told them, like your mother told you."

"Unless he used the Jedi thing to make them forget."

I shuddered. "He gets creepier the more I try to figure him out."

"Agreed. But the fact that a... great-great-granddaughter of his is around, is bound to be big news. If you want it to be, that is. If you don't... I won't say anything."

I was about to thank him for his discretion, when I remembered something. "I... may have mentioned it to Luke last night."

He leaned in, his shoulder nudging mine. "Well then, I hate to tell you, but they're all going to know soon. I'm surprised I didn't hear it through the grapevine already. A lot of people are probably going to get a lot more interested in you than they already were."

"Why…" I stopped myself. "People already knew I was related to someone, didn't they? Luke said he could see it. That was why that Winston was asking me questions – to see if I knew. Did you know? Right away, I mean?"

"It's not quite as straightforward as that – not for me, at least," he said. "I could just tell there was something different about you. It's not like there was a spotlight shining on your head or anything, but there's something there. It's like… you know when you're driving in the summer, when it's really hot, and you look down the highway and you can see the air kind of shimmering? Not like that exactly, but it's subtle. But yeah, people will have noticed. Claire and Ben have, and obviously Luke did too, and there's been others, keeping an eye on you. When they find out that you know, though… things may come to a bit of a head."

"Is it going to be bad?"

"Nah, I don't think so. It'll be a big deal, but it'll be fine." He patted my leg. "And don't worry. I've got your back."

"Thanks."

CHAPTER TWENTY-EIGHT

The next few nights, I felt self-conscious among the magicians. But it seemed that, so far, nothing had changed. On Friday evening, I found out why.

"Luke hasn't said anything," Eric said, appearing out of nowhere as he was apt to do, and falling into step with me.

"I thought you said he'd tell everyone."

He glanced over his shoulder. "I caught up with him the other night, and asked him to keep it to himself. He's probably told a few of the other kids – and they'll all find out eventually – but no sense in encouraging it."

I turned and looked at him. "Why are you keeping it quiet?"

"To give you some time. To see… well, to see what happens. I've got to get going." Giving my arm a squeeze, he turned to go; just then, a woman came hurrying up to us.

"Eric," she said, her eyes darting towards me. "Is this the girl who went to talk to Raffaele?" Her tone was hushed, serious.

I cleared my throat. "Yes. I'm Heather," I said, rather more loudly than strictly necessary.

As if I hadn't spoken, she continued. "He wants to see her. Now."

"She's standing right here," Eric pointed out. "You don't have to tell me, Stasia."

"Eric." Her voice dropped lower. "He's dying."

"Hasn't he been dying for ten years?"

Stasia looked shocked at his indifference. "Now. He's dying now. We might already be too late. It may be nothing to you, but he asked to see her, and I'm supposed to take her to him. Now."

Eric looked at me. "Do you want to go? This isn't a police state."

Part of me wanted to shake my head and walk away, to continue to the silver tent and watch Luke perform. But I had to admit that I was curious as to why Raffaele would summon me at the eleventh hour. And I supposed he was the only great-grandparent I had left. I followed Stasia, though she looked as though she would rather I had not.

We came into the house and found it full of light and people – a dramatic change from all the other evenings when it had appeared empty and lifeless. It was quiet, though: a vigil. I saw Luke standing against a wall, his face serious and pale, holding the hand of a woman who had to be his mother; the silver tent would stay dark tonight. There had to be three dozen people here – probably a third of the magicians were packed into this little house. They must all be related to him – all distant cousins of mine somehow, I realized.

Isabella came out of the side chamber and looked straight at me, before looking round the room. "He wishes to be here, with all of you."

Without a word, a muscular, grey-haired man followed her into the room. A few minutes later, he carried out the frail form of the ancient man and arranged him gently on a couch, covering him with a blanket. Raffaele looked, if anything, more lively than he had on my prior visits; I wondered if they were mistaken about his imminent passing. He laid his bony hand on the head of the man who had carried him, and murmured something I couldn't make out.

As if on cue, each person in the room approached, one by one, the older generations first. By the time the first few people had passed, I realized what this must be: he was saying his goodbyes, giving his blessing, just as Granny Chrissie once had. He had his whole family gathered around him. And me.

Unsure of what my role in this affair was to be, I stayed back, leaning against the door; I had hardly taken two steps in. But when everyone else had had their moment, he turned his head and pointed to me. "Heather Ross. Come here, child."

I approached cautiously, trying not to flinch when he took my hand. His skin was clammy, his hand all bone and sinew. He held my gaze a moment, then addressed the room. "This girl child, Heather, I claim as my great-granddaughter."

"But..." I looked down at him.

He actually laughed a little. "I can see that you know it," he said, more quietly, speaking only to me now. "And I knew you the moment you first came to see me. I can see my sweet Chrissie, and jolly Miss Ross, both, when I look at your face. How fitting that the fates brought their children together. I wronged them both, and it is too late to ask forgiveness."

Raising his voice again, he continued. "Mine is not the only blood that runs in her veins. Her great-grandmother was the daughter of Sébastien." The others in the room were no longer troubling to hide their whispers; I heard the name repeated in hushed tones. So much for keeping things quiet. Raffaele was still holding on to my hand, but his grip was weakening. "As he gave me his blessing long ago, I pass it on to his successor. Lean down, child," he added, raising his other hand. "Sébastien's blessing, and mine." I bent down as requested, and he pressed his thumb to the centre of my forehead, murmuring something under his breath. It might have been my imagination, but I thought I felt a chill at the spot, a tingling sensation.

I had no time to consider this, however. Still holding my hand, Raffaele let his other hand drop to the blanket. "I have been... fortunate... beyond what I deserved. I am ready to rest, now."

His eyes closed. His chest rose and fell in one shallow breath, another, and then was still. It seemed there was a shimmer in the air around him for a second, but it might have been a trick of my eyes; then I felt as if a cold wind had blown past. The hand in mine was lifeless.

Letting go, I took several steps back as Isabella rushed to Raffaele's side, breaking into sobs. Others of the family approached as well, gathering round the body that had finally given up its lengthy grasp on life. I felt indecent, a spectator to their grief, and I sidled away toward the door.

At the last minute, Luke took hold of my forearm. He looked pale and shaken, but tearless. "You really are one of us. Don't go."

"It's not my place," I whispered. "I shouldn't be here. I shouldn't..." Shaking my head, I slipped out the door.

Despite my opinion of the man, I had to admit that at least he had known he was in the wrong, and I was touched that he had wanted to give me his blessing. But it should not have been me who was with him at the last moment. It should have been Isabella, his daughter, or any of the others who had shared some portion of his life; all I shared was a small fraction of my DNA.

I could have turned back up the lane, through the archway and towards the tents, but instead I walked out along the dark road, needing to be in a place of quiet. Although I had been with Granny Chrissie very near her end, I had never before seen someone actually die, much less while they were holding my hand; I felt changed by it, somehow.

The night was cool, and there was a light fog drifting in and out, but I felt colder than the weather should have made me, as if a rivulet of icy water were falling on the top of my head and flowing over my skull, down my spine and limbs. I felt displaced, light, unattached to the ground. Fearing that I might be about to faint, I sat down on a rock by the side of the road, wondering if I would be able to make it the remaining couple of hundred metres back to Kestrel Cottage under my own power.

When I heard a call of my name, it sounded unnaturally loud, almost echoing in my head. "I'm here," I replied, only able to raise my voice so far.

Eric came jogging up out of the darkness. "Are you alright?" Definitely too loud.

"I don't think so." I crunched my eyes shut, rubbed them a bit, and tried looking at him again. I definitely wasn't seeing quite right; there appeared to be some sort of halo around him. "I'm not feeling very well. I think I might be having some kind of a weird migraine."

He put his arm around me and helped me to my feet. "Maybe. And you've had a bit of a shock." Clearly, word was already spreading. "Come on, let's get you home."

CHAPTER TWENTY-NINE

When I woke up on Saturday morning, I was still not quite myself. It was as if I had had too much sugar, or caffeine; I felt like I was vibrating slightly. The light-headedness had passed, though, which was a relief. It was only upon getting out of bed that I realized I was still in my sweater and jeans from the night before.

While changing into clean clothes, I realized that I could smell toast. Wasn't that supposed to be a sign of having a stroke? I was sure I had read that somewhere. But no, that was definitely toast. Coming out of the bedroom, I found Eric in the kitchen.

"Were you here all night?"

He jumped a little at the sound of my voice. "I hope that's okay. You seemed really out of it by the time we got here, so I just crashed on the couch. I didn't want to leave you alone. Are you feeling better?"

"Yes, a bit. Maybe," I amended. "I don't feel like I'm going to pass out any more, and your voice sounds normal – it didn't last night – but I still feel kind of off, somehow. I can't quite put my finger on it. I'm not sure if my eyes have stopped playing tricks on me, or if it's just that it's light out now."

"Sit down." He passed me a plate of toast and a glass of juice.

"Something to eat will probably help. And maybe you should tell me exactly what happened last night."

"I wasn't drinking, or anything," I said, as a preamble. "I assume you've heard that he died?"

There was no need to elaborate on who I was talking about, which was a good thing, as I didn't really want to say his name. Eric just nodded. "I heard."

"Did they tell you that he told everyone there about me? And that he died right after talking to me? He was still holding my hand when he…" I let it trail off.

His brow furrowed. "No wonder you were in shock. What did he say to you?"

Taking a deep breath, I launched into a full account of events, beginning when I had walked away with Stasia. It was all still vivid in my mind, and I tried to include every detail, no matter how trivial. Eric mostly just listened, though he asked for clarification on a few points.

"So, he gave you his blessing and Sébastien's… do you remember how exactly he said it?"

I thought back. "He said that Sébastien had blessed him a long time ago, and he was passing it on to me because I was his successor. Along with his own blessing."

"And then what?"

"Then he touched my forehead, here," I replied, pointing to the spot. "It felt kind of cold, but the whole situation was so weird, I don't really know. And then… he said he was more fortunate than he deserved…"

"True."

"Yeah. And then he said he was ready to rest, and he just… closed his eyes and died. It was as if he was finished, and chose to do it."

Eric leaned across the table. "And did you see anything

unusual, then?"

I debated for a moment. "I don't know. I thought I did, at the time — something kind of wavering in the air, and a chill — but then I felt so much worse afterwards, it may have just been the migraine or whatever coming on."

"Maybe. Maybe not." He got up and went to look out the window, towards the stones. "I've never seen anyone die, so I don't really know, but they say... They say that when a magician dies, you can see their spirit, or their soul, or whatever."

It was the idea that had been hanging around the fringes of my mind, but I'd been unwilling to let it in. "Don't some people say that about when anyone dies?"

"Yeah. I don't know what I believe, but after about half my life with this travelling circus, I've learned not to dismiss anything too quickly. What I do know is that people here put a lot of importance on the whole deathbed blessing thing. The fact that you started feeling strange right after it happened..." He lapsed into silence for a few seconds. "Look, don't listen to me; I'm just thinking out loud. You should probably talk to somebody who understands this all better than I do. Do you want me to call Ben?"

I wasn't ready yet to face the people who had been in the death-room, but Eric was right: it would be good to get some answers, if there were any to be had. When I nodded, he pulled out his phone and sent a quick text; a response came within a couple of minutes.

"He'll meet us at the stones in half an hour, but he says I should take you there straight away. Are you up for it?"

A light misty drizzle had set in, barely enough to be called rain, but the fresh air helped clear my head a little when we stepped outside. As I paused to zip up my jacket, I noticed Eric looking at me strangely. "What?"

"I think I'm getting a better idea of what might be going on.

Ben will know for sure, but…" He looked around for a moment, then nodded discreetly toward a man walking up the road with a dog. "Do you see anything strange when you look at them?"

I looked, trying to figure out what I was supposed to be seeing. They had clearly been out for a while; the dog's fur was slicked down with damp, as was the man's grey hair. He nodded as he passed, and greeted us in Gaelic. I remembered my *madainn mhath* in reply, but still could not see what the point of this exercise was. "Nothing. I don't see anything odd at all," I said quietly, once the man was out of earshot.

"Okay. Now look at me. I'll stand back a bit."

Accordingly, I looked at Eric, initially just taking stock of the details as I had with the man and dog. His jacket was zipped up to the neck, his hands in the pockets of his jeans, damp hair pushed back off his face; his expression was neutral, maybe curious, as he watched me sizing him up. If this was some kind of a riddle, I didn't get it.

The sound of car tires made me glance away, and as I did, there was something just at the periphery of my vision. What was it? I looked past Eric in the other direction, and yes, there was definitely something. I had seen it the night before, I realized, and chalked it up to some kind of visual disturbance. "There's… kind of a… not a halo, exactly. It's like an aura. I can only see it if I look quickly."

His whole expression changed in an instant: a huge grin, his eyes alight, he could have passed for half his real age. "I knew it. Come on."

He was walking fast; I needed to almost jog to keep up with his long strides around the corner of the road and up to the back gate of the standing stones. Given the weather, I was surprised to see that it was quite busy; it must be a tour bus. "Tell me what you see."

"Just… lots of people. Nothing weird. Wait…" Over by the

central stone, I could see someone; from the back, she would have looked indistinguishable from the other visitors but for a slight trick of the light that made her look as if she was illuminated more brightly than the others. When she turned and pushed back the hood of her coat, I recognized her as the woman who often sat in the ticket booth for the magicians. "Am I…?" That was it, exactly; when I looked back at Eric, I saw him in the same almost imperceptible light. "I'm starting to see what you see. I can tell you apart from regular people."

It was exciting for a moment, but then I frowned. What exactly had Raffaele done to me?

"You already could, though," Eric pointed out, maybe guessing what I was thinking. "A week ago, you picked everyone out of the crowd."

I shook my head. "This is different. It's not just a gut feeling; I can actually see something. It's a bit like what you said – like a heat mirage over the road in the summer. He did something to me."

"Maybe he just showed you something you already had."

As I was pondering this, Ben came through the gate. "How are you, darling?" he asked, giving me a hug. "I've heard your name a few times already this morning. I'd like to hear the story in your words, if you're up for it. Here, these tourists look like they're clearing off; come over and lean up a bit against this last stone, you look pale."

I had already experienced how touching the stones could be oddly calming, but this was another sensation altogether. The energy that had been running around my veins all morning had suddenly found an outlet, it seemed: or rather, I felt as if I had been wired in to something that could direct that energy into its proper channel. "It's different, isn't it?" Eric said, shooting Ben a look.

Ben held up a hand. "Don't worry about that just now. What happened last night?"

Taking a deep breath, I recounted the story again, remembering to fill in details on the things that Eric had asked questions about. "I had wondered about you, I really had," Ben said at last, shaking his head. "And it all makes more sense now. But it's shocking, all the same."

A woman with a large camera walked past and gave me a dirty look; mindful suddenly of what I was doing, I took two steps away from the stone, already missing the sensation of contact with it. Once she had passed by, I looked at the two men in front of me. "That's great. Any chance that anyone could make it make sense for me?"

"I'll make it very simple," Ben replied. "You've got the gift, Heather. I suspected as much when I met you, though I couldn't think where you could have got it from; I thought maybe you were one of those occasional ones that get it out of nowhere. But Sébastien... he was a right bastard, by all accounts, but as a magician? He was like the five-hundred-year storm. I only saw him twice – I was just a boy when he died – but it makes sense that his blood would still mean something, even four generations on. And Raffaele was no slouch, either, when he was still healthy. The best of us right now would be hard pressed to match him. Do you know how Sébastien died?" When I nodded, he went on. "He was shot just outside his tent, and Raffaele was the first to run to him; with his last breath, Sébastien blessed him. They say that that was when Raffaele became a truly great illusionist; he was talented already, but something of Sébastien passed on to him."

I felt again the sensation of Raffaele pressing his cold, bony thumb to my skin. "And you're saying... that he passed that on to me?"

Ben held out his hands. "I can't pretend to know every mystery under the sun, but I'm sure Raffaele believed that he did. He cared for family – you saw how he gathered them all round him at the last – and even though Sébastien never really did, it would make sense that Raffaele would want the legacy to pass on to his only descendant."

"But I'm not," I said, shaking my head. "I'm not his only descendant. Everyone says he seduced women everywhere; there must have been plenty of kids. Even in my own family… my Granny Chrissie had two kids, and then grandchildren and great-grandchildren. I've got a sister and cousins who've all got Raffaele's DNA as well, into the bargain. Why me?"

"Do you see any of them here?" Ben asked, with a shrug. "Would any of them want to be here?"

"You said your great-grandmother only told you," Eric added. "She must have had her reasons."

Ben was right; I was the only one who'd ever been much interested in our roots. As to whether Granny Chrissie had told me about the magicians because I was interested, or whether the secret of her parentage had given her the ability to see something in me: that was harder to say, but they were both right. Most of my family would have been dismissing all of this as superstitious nonsense at best.

The question had apparently been rhetorical, for Ben continued. "Now here's where we get to the things that probably no one has told you. So the gift tends to go through bloodlines, but it's not a perfect science, you see. It pops up sometimes in people like Sébastien – and Raffaele as well, for that matter – who've got no background that we know of. But it doesn't run in every member of a family, either. It's like…" He paused a moment. "Like being left-handed, or having perfect pitch, it sometimes jumps around, right? Most of the families here, if both parents are magicians, chances are most of their kids will be, too, but not always. Did you know Luke has an older sister who works as a nursery teacher in Milton Keynes? She grew up here same as he did, but never had more than a glimmer of the talent. She went her own way when she was grown, though she's no less a part of the family – and who knows, maybe down the road her kids'll come back to us, magicians themselves."

I thought back to first-year biology. "Some people are carriers, without having the trait themselves." If I conceived of it as a DNA exercise, I could come to grips with it better.

He looked pleased. "That's it, exactly. So somehow, you've wound up with the right formula, and maybe it just needed that boost to bring it to light. Because everything you've said about what happened when you left the house... it fits. Some of us have it straight from birth, but most have it kind of woken up some time later. And especially when you've grown up not knowing about it – well, it stands to reason it might be a bit of a shock to the system."

"I'll say," Eric added, pointing toward Ben. "The first time he proved to me that I could really do this stuff, I seem to remember my first response was to lose my lunch."

Ben chuckled, but then grew serious. "Now here's the other thing. I know you've only just started to figure this out, but you've a decision in front of you, sooner or later."

"Whether to join you, or not." The import of the words resolved in my brain after they had already come out of my mouth.

He nodded. "You can't be expected to have an answer to that now, or even soon. None of us know what you're capable of, and only you can say what's back home that you want to go back to, or not. I expect Eric's told you he took a few months to make up his mind. Some take even longer. But given what's happened – there may be some who aren't willing to give you that luxury. There's going to be some who are looking for an answer tonight."

"Tonight?" Two weeks ago, I still hadn't been a hundred per cent sure that these magicians truly existed, at least in the way they'd been described to me by Granny Chrissie. It was beyond surreal that there was even a suggestion that I might become one of them – that I might in fact be one of them already. "I wasn't even sure I'm up to going tonight."

"Oh, you'll have to go tonight, darling," Ben said, his accent more pronounced than usual. "We'll all have to. It's the wake."

CHAPTER THIRTY

I'd never been to a magician's wake. I'd never been to anyone's wake, and only a handful of funerals. I had no idea what to expect. Half of my wardrobe was black, and I'd packed a skirt in the bottom of my bag, so at least I felt that I was dressed appropriately, but I walked down to the field that night with rather the sensation of walking into a lion's den.

To my surprise, I found that at first glance, the show was going on just as on any other night, the road lined with cars, the field full of merry, unsuspecting visitors. But each of the magicians I saw wore a black armband, and each of them – even Eric, who I knew had held no great opinion of Raffaele as a person – had changed their performance so that in some way, it paid tribute to the deceased. I had known of Raffaele only in relation to Granny Chrissie – and, later, to myself – and apart from her description, I really knew little of what kind of magician he had been, but I felt I was learning something of it as I walked from tent to tent.

At the centre of the field, where the menagerie usually stood, was a midnight blue marquee. This reference, at least, I recognized. Stepping inside, I found myself in an overgrown garden, almost a maze. It was hard to remember that it was an illusion; I felt the branches brush my arms, smelled the heady perfume of the night-blooming flowers that dropped petals gently on the ground as I walked past. Coming at last to the end, after several wrong turns, I came next into something like a ruined temple. Sand was under foot, and in some places where I actually had to clamber over fallen pillars I could have sworn that their faded pictographs had been warmed by the sun just moments before. Next were the shattered walls of a church, or cathedral, with the rain splashing my face as it poured in from the open sky. It defied belief that there was still a tent roof between me and the clear night of the real world. This was their message, their mourning for a man who had been family to so many of them.

By the time I reached the centre of the tent, I had already guessed what I might find there, but it took my breath away all the same: I pushed through a feather-light drape of silk and found myself stepping into the vast nothingness of space. My feet registered that the ground was still solid beneath me, but my eyes told a different story. As far as I could see in any direction – left, right, in front, behind, up, and, most disconcertingly, down – there was nothing but a deep blue-blackness filled with stars. I was sure I was not the only person in the tent, but it was just the distant murmur of voices that helped me remember that I was still connected to the earth.

Taking an uncertain step, I moved forward and found that I did not fall, but with each moment I was less aware of the ground. It seemed as if I could go in any direction or dimension, coming closer to distant stars, running the tips of my fingers through the pale stripe of the Milky Way. I wondered if the whole family had come together to conjure it; if Raffaele had been capable of this on his own, he must have been extraordinary indeed.

I had no idea how long I spent there – it only seemed like minutes – but at some point I felt a hand wrap round mine. Eric was there, and suddenly the grass had returned beneath my feet, the stars now gracing an arc overhead as if we were outdoors. "It's time," he said, letting go of my hand as the scene resolved into merely a tent. "Are you ready to face the music?"

Of course, this could not be all there was to it. "I guess so."

When we emerged, I could see that more time had passed than I had realized. The quarter-moon that had been low in the west had long set, and all the tents were dark now except for one, the deep purple one where the magicians' ceilidh had been held the Saturday before. Dozens of people were filing in, but Eric pulled me aside. "Don't let it get to you, whatever happens in there."

"Is it going to be bad?" I had anticipated stares and whispers, but not a confrontation.

"Honestly? I don't know how people are going to be." He stood back, pushing his hair off his face with both hands, and I noticed for the first time that he had dressed up for the occasion: black trousers and waistcoat and a crisp white shirt. "There's been talk, for sure. A couple of people have asked me questions, since they know we're friends. But then a couple of people have shut up really quick when I've walked in, for the same reason."

"I hear that wakes usually involve a fair bit of drinking," I said. "So I guess people may wind up speaking their minds before the evening's out."

Eric gave me a hug. "It'll be okay in the end. It's just that it's not often any more that people like you turn up – outsiders becoming part of this. I think it was more common way back, but since I joined, there's been three, maybe four people. You'd be news even without everything else."

"And you think I should? Stay, I mean… join you guys."

"It's your decision." He stepped back again. "But I know I've never regretted it. Look, we'll talk more about that later, but right now we'd better go in."

To my surprise, my first impression of the wake was that it was not so very much different than the party, except for the lack of dancing and the notable inclusion of a long trestle table with a simple wooden coffin on it. Some people were approaching the deceased, like a visitation at a funeral home, but the overall atmosphere was far from sombre, and a good number of the company had drinks in hand.

"Is this what every magician's funeral is like, or is it like this because it's what he would have wanted?" I asked quietly, accepting a glass of something.

"Bit of both, I'm thinking," Eric replied. "I haven't seen many, but people here have a tendency to die at some pretty advanced ages."

"A hundred and thirty-eight; no kidding."

He ignored my editorial comment. "And, not to be callous, but there's only so sad you can be about someone who dies when they're really old. Whatever you say about the guy, he had a fuller life than most people on the planet."

This was certainly true. A few people were holding forth with stories about Raffaele's life, and I listened in here and there, mostly staying around the fringes of things. So far, it was going better than I had feared. The first cracks didn't begin to appear until about three-quarters of an hour in. Eric had excused himself briefly, leaving me on my own, but I spotted a familiar face in Luke. The moment I approached him, the two other young men he'd been talking to pointedly turned their backs and walked away.

"That bad, is it?" I asked.

Luke looked so uncomfortable that I felt quite sorry for him. "You have managed to cause some drama. Not that it'd be a first for this family," he added, "but still. Some people think you timed your moment on purpose."

"How could I have timed anything? I spent most of my life not even sure you people were real; I only found out five days ago that I was related to any of you. And it was him that sent for me on his deathbed, not me showing up unannounced."

"Hey, hey." He raised both his hands. "You're preaching to

the converted here, cousin. I believe you. I'm just saying, don't take it too personally if people are... well, like that," he said, pointing in the direction the two others had gone. "Give it a few days and things'll calm down. Those two don't even have an opinion of their own, anyhow – but Isabella's their gran, and she's got opinions enough for the whole place." A strange expression came over his face just then, and he mumbled a curse under his breath. I had a feeling I knew who was standing behind me.

"What is she doing here?"

Yes, it was definitely Isabella. I took a deep breath and deliberately waited to turn around, though I heard Granny Chrissie's voice in my head saying *Who's 'she', the cat's mother?*, as I had so often been told as a child. "I only came to..."

"You have no gift. You have no part in this family," she spat, as if laying a curse on me. "And you had no right to be standing with my Papa at his dying breath, after all the years I cared for him!"

"I've got no need to stand here and be told off when I was just trying to be polite and pay my respects," I replied, rather surprising myself. "I'm sorry for your loss."

As I turned to go, I heard Isabella say to Luke, in a voice clearly intended for me to hear, "We don't need any more *trovatelli* here."

I walked away, idly wishing I knew Italian, but I was certain it wasn't complimentary, whatever it meant. Although I was sorely tempted to leave – after all, I hadn't really known the man, and I wasn't part of the corps of magicians - part of me didn't want to give Isabella the satisfaction; instead I kept my eyes peeled for Eric, or Claire, or anyone else who might be more inclined to give me the time of day. I passed Winston, who was watching me speculatively, eyes narrowed, and Stasia who seemed almost in a panic to avoid having to talk to me. Finally, I found Ben, sat down beside him in silence, and finished the drink I'd been holding on to for the past thirty minutes.

These people were bereaved, I reminded myself, and they did have a point, even if they didn't all have their facts entirely straight. I was an interloper, and I hadn't begun to process any of it yet, much less figure out where my own plans lay, on a spectrum from Isabella's disdain to Ben's and Eric's barely-contained enthusiasm. It seemed that every question answered opened up ten more to be asked.

CHAPTER THIRTY-ONE

Sunday dawned with high winds and all the pent-up rain that we'd been lucky to escape in the past week. It was weather conducive to shutting oneself up indoors, and I did exactly that, making a pot of tea and sitting by the window, looking out at the rolling clouds. I was exhausted, not just from the night before but from the whole week, the weight of all the revelations that had fallen upon me. I needed to stop thinking about it for a few minutes, so I just listened to the rhythm of the rain on the roof slates and watched the pattern of the drops running down the glass.

After a while, perhaps from sitting still too long, I started to feel a tingling in my limbs – not that they were falling asleep, exactly, but something made me get up from the chair. Flexing my fingers a little, I laid my palm on the window glass. It was cold at first, but quickly warmed from my body heat. It was only after a couple of minutes that I noticed a pattern: it looked as if every drop was skirting around the contour of my fingers. I watched this for a moment, amused at the illusion, before taking my hand away.

There, on the glass, was the outline of my hand – without a drop of rain on it. It only lasted a second before the water ran down and filled it back in, but I knew what I had seen. Pulling on my raincoat, I hastened down the road to Flora's.

I was glad to see Claire answer the door; it made things easier. "Do you know where Eric is?"

She smiled. "Out along the main road toward Breasclete, the grey house past the church. But I can just text him, and save you the trouble." Her phone was already in her hand as she said it, and a beep sounded moments later. "He'll come by in twenty minutes." Over her shoulder, I saw Colleen's mouth tighten into a straight line for a moment.

"Tell him to meet me at the cottage, will you?" I said.

He was there in fifteen, and I gave a brief explanation of what had happened, but dismissed his comments on it for the moment. "I don't know what the hell it was, and I couldn't replicate it just now when I tried. But I need to know how this starts."

"I think that's what you just saw, on the window. It's different for everyone…"

"No." I cut him off. "I don't mean that. I mean… when you came here – or wherever it was – and Ben convinced you to join them, what did you do? How did you learn it? How did… how did people treat you?"

"Does that mean you're thinking of staying?" he asked, pulling out a chair and sitting down backwards on it.

"No. I mean… I don't know. I need to know more about what I might be getting myself into, before I can even think about that. Even you have to admit, it's a pretty ridiculous thing to contemplate."

"Totally ridiculous," he agreed. "But so are a lot of things. Okay, so I won't try to give you a sales pitch… yet. Which question am I supposed to answer first?"

I thought about it, and about what had happened the night before. "How did people react? I mean, I know Colleen wasn't thrilled, but other than that."

He took a deep breath. "It was a bit different, obviously, since there wasn't the whole drama with somebody dying, and all these long-lost connections. My mom had given me Ben's name, he remembered her very well, my birthday matches up, and I even look a fair bit like him: that much was kind of a no-brainer. The business with him having a new family – well, that would have been an uncomfortable situation whether magic was involved or not. I think I was just at the tail end of the illegitimate kids, so to speak."

"Ben's?"

"No, no, I mean in general. It was... not like it was something that happened every day – someone like me turning up – but overall there was a bit of an 'oh, this again'. I got the sense that people expected that this happened every now and then. But look at when I was born, just at the beginning of the sixties. Birth control gets to be a thing, and suddenly there aren't so many girls left with souvenirs after the magicians come to town. I'm kind of digressing here, but the point is, it wasn't an everyday thing then, but it's much less now."

I nodded. "Yeah, I get that. You're not the only one who's told me. But how did people act about it?"

He glanced out the window. "Ben's parents were pretty excited. Lots of the younger people were really welcoming, probably partly because I'm American, which makes me a novelty, same as you. They're a pretty diverse bunch, but we never perform outside of Europe, not as a group, and that's kind of determined who winds up connected to them. Some people were not so welcoming, although they weren't horrible to me – more of a 'really, another bastard?' kind of thing, or waiting for me to prove myself. That one's kind of a given for anybody, even if it's someone who's grown up here and they're graduating to actually participating in the show, but more so for outsiders."

"But you're not an outsider now."

"Yes and no. I'll never be as immersed in it as somebody like Luke, who's been in this his whole life and has no particular desire to leave. But you're right, over time they got used to me." He chuckled, shaking his head slightly. "The interesting part was deciding what to do with myself the first time there was a break – obviously, we don't do this three-hundred-sixty-five days a year. I had two months to fill, and I was weirdly afraid to go back home; I guess I was afraid all this might disappear or something."

"So what did you do?"

"A couple of guys said they had a place in London and that I should join them. It was a squat, really – all kinds of people coming and going all the time – but there was this great creative energy, people making music, painting on the walls, that sort of thing. As a kid I'd always wanted to be an artist, so I gave it a go. It's my real-world thing, but not too 'real world', you know?"

"Wow." I wasn't sure that it had completely occurred to me to think that they all must have some degree of life outside of this. "And did you ever go home?"

"Of course I did. It's not an exile. After that first time – and once I had money for a plane ticket – I went back for a visit: got rid of some stuff I didn't need, sold my car, that sort of thing. I go back about once a year or so. My family is still my family."

"And do they know what it is you do?"

"No," he said immediately. "That's one challenge. As far as my parents know, I'm an artist who travels a lot. It's not a lie. But... Heather, whatever you wind up deciding, it's important – part of what makes all this work is keeping it a bit out of the public eye. It gets harder and harder these days, with social media and everything else – Eleanor and Ari are good at jamming people from taking photos in the tents, texting from here, that sort of thing, but there's whole websites of people trying to track us."

I was all too conscious of how I had narrowed down where they would be. "Is that such a bad thing?"

He shrugged. "Honestly? I think it's kind of fun. Between you and me, I sometimes post to throw people off the trail. But there needs to be some kind of mystery."

"Don't worry. I'm not going to tell anyone about it."

"I know. I wouldn't have… I figured I could trust you, from the start. And you can trust me. I wouldn't be suggesting you come with us if I really thought you were going to have a bad time of it. We've got a week and a half till… well, till things come to a head here. I think we can teach you a few things between now and then."

CHAPTER THIRTY-TWO

The next day, I decided I had to get away – get out of Callanish, just for a few hours, to think more clearly about all of it. I had heard that there was a remote beach at Dalbeg; that sounded like the right sort of place to sort my head out.

Getting off the bus on a windswept, deserted-looking stretch of road, I made my way down the laneway and over a cattle grid. Ahead of me, two gentle hills rolled down into a tiny bay. The road curved past three or four houses and a couple of bored-looking black cows, before petering out at a few picnic tables and a footpath leading down to the beach.

I sat down on a rock, watching the waves roll in and out; the waters that had looked so placid from a distance were actually quite wild, and the tide was rising. After a while, the farthest inroad of the waves came within a few feet of my perch. On a whim, I moved closer and made a handprint in the sand, then watched the next wave wash it away, thinking of the window and the raindrops. How on earth did people go from that sort of thing to the performances I had seen?

And how on earth had I come, in the space of a year, from being a normal, nine-to-five, home-owning, married grownup – albeit with a few offbeat interests – to being a magician's descendant twice over, maybe possessed of some tiny inkling of a gift, and seriously considering running away with the circus? There were so many variables that had had to fall into place to result in my being here. If nothing else, I was still a bit baffled that Granny Chrissie's daughter – my gran – had managed to wind up marrying Ina's son with no one being the wiser. I had never been one to believe in that sort of thing, but it did have a distinct feeling of fate about it.

I spent a couple of hours at the beach – partly out of necessity, due to the infrequency of the bus service – and by the time I set out to go, I did feel calmer. A light mist had set in, but it was just enough to be refreshing; I didn't even bother to pull my raincoat from my bag as I made my way back up the lane to the bus stop.

When the bus came around and stopped for me, though, the driver stared as I came aboard. "How did you manage to stay so dry, then?" he asked, after taking my fare.

"What do you mean?" I laughed a bit, looking around – but then noticed that the two ladies in the front seats looked like poor drowned rats; a storm must have somehow blown through on a different course and skipped Dalbeg. Except that then I looked at the windscreen.

It was pouring down, the kind of cats-and-dogs rain that should have soaked me through, standing at that windy corner with no coat or shelter. And yet I was barely damp. All I could do was smile and take a seat.

I was definitely going to have to get someone to show me how to use this.

CHAPTER THIRTY-THREE

"Try again, darling." Despite my decided lack of results, Ben showed no sign of annoyance. "It took him far longer to make anything happen, don't worry."

"Maybe this is enough for today," Eric suggested. It was Thursday afternoon, and they had been attempting to give me some sort of magical training for the past three days, to no noticeable effect.

I was restless: too alert and yet tired at the same time. Things seemed to be growing more hectic at the performances in the evenings, and I was all too aware of the attention I drew from some of the magicians. Between that and the fruitless attempts to make something of this talent I was supposed to have, I wasn't sleeping much. "I'm useless," I admitted. "It feels like the harder I try to grasp at it, the more it disappears. Maybe I need to go back to that beach or something."

Ben patted me on the back. "Go down to the stones for a bit tonight. It's too mad with tour buses right now."

It was his solution to everything, it seemed. Calm down: go to the stones. Not feeling well: go to the stones. Complete ineptitude at magic: yes, go to the stones. I was about to make some kind of smart-ass remark when it hit me.

"That's where it comes from, isn't it? You get your powers from the stones. That's why you come here, of all places."

The two men looked at each other. "Sort of…" said Eric.

"Not exactly," Ben countered at almost the same moment. "Where we get our gifts from – well, there's genetics, but why that works or where it originally come from, who knows. The magic, it's somewhere inside, but these stones, and the Avebury stones, and the Rocher des Doms, and most of the other places we go – that's the recharge for our batteries, so to speak. So I suppose it is where we get power, in some sense of the word, now I think about it. And when that power source gets itself charged up… well, of all the places and times you could have stumbled upon us, you picked the right one."

"It's the moon thing, isn't it? That's why you only come here every eighteen or nineteen years." They had never asked exactly how I had come to figure out that they would be here, but Eric at least had to know by now that it was more than just a lucky happenstance. "There's something about it, that makes the stones more powerful."

"Right in one," Ben replied, and said no more on the subject.

Eric chimed in, once we had started out toward the stones and left the older man behind. "It must seem strange to most people, when we roll up with this extravagant show in a tiny village that probably has less than a hundred people."

"There's probably only a few thousand in the whole island," I replied. "So, yeah. And it had occurred to me to wonder how you all support yourself and afford all this travelling around, but that's none of my business."

He slowed his pace a little. "It might be your business. We do the things we need to keep going in the weird mystical sense, like coming here, and then we do the things we need to keep going in the 'food to eat and clothes on our backs' sense. I'm not the only one who has a day job, but a lot of them just do this. We go to big performance events – the Edinburgh Festival, some of the big German Christmas fairs… about half of us even made a pretty good go of it last year in London, when the Olympics were on. But we never take the whole show – the tents, everything – into cities. It just doesn't work there, but a handful of us busking as part of something bigger, where we don't prompt too many questions? It's another way to keep the wolf from the door, and it's fun."

We walked along in silence for a minute or two. There were calculations going on in my head that I was trying to avoid making; for once in my life I wanted to just go on instinct. "I envy your ability to just pick up and do all that," I said eventually. "Just walk away. I've never been very good at taking risks."

"What are you talking about? You took a risk coming here. What if you'd been wrong about us?"

I made a vague hand gesture. "I would have just had a nice vacation."

"Bullshit." He stepped out in front, turned to face me, and stopped, forcing me to stop as well. "This is going to sound incredibly cocky, and I don't mean it that way, but you're not going to tell me that after however many years wondering about all this, it wouldn't have been a crushing disappointment if there had been nothing here? Or if we were just some lame sideshow that didn't live up to your great-grandma's memories? I took a risk based on a story, too, so don't act like I don't know what I'm talking about. You're more of a risk-taker than you think. Hell," he added, his tone lighter now, "you accepted a drink from Luke. That's a gamble even I'm leery of. Now come on."

When we got to the standing stones, the tour buses were just pulling away, leaving the site relatively quiet. Eric didn't offer any suggestions as to what I should do, so I approached the stones on my own; I tried to visualize the energy that was apparently charged in the megaliths, but couldn't quite do it. So instead, I decided to walk round the whole site, slowly, investigating each individual slab of gneiss – something I hadn't really done since my very first visit. I pretended they were people who I was being introduced to for the very first time, and came to see that each stone did have its own personality as well as distinct appearance.

After a while, I realized that though I could not see the energy, I could feel it – almost hear it but not quite – like the vibration that goes along with something very loud and low. If I paid enough attention, and wasn't distracted by the passing of other visitors, I started to notice that each stone had its own frequency as well. This had to be a good thing. If I was aware of the energy, if I could sense it, then perhaps eventually I could learn to work with it.

Reaching my hand out to a stone surface, I did not touch it, but held my palm an inch or two away and waited. Eventually, I thought there was something – a tingling, maybe. I tried another stone, not in the avenue this time, but in the central ring. This was stronger, definitely. What about the tallest stone? Just as I was about to move toward it, though, Eric caught my wrist.

"Not yet." I must have looked at him strangely, because he leaned in closer. "You've got the right idea. But you'll want to come back to that when there aren't so many people around."

CHAPTER THIRTY-FOUR

The moon was waxing, giving more light than it had a week earlier, and before it set for the night I slipped away from the magicians' tents and back to the standing stones. At this hour, there was no one here: the tourists were long gone, and all the magicians were still performing.

Seeing the stones was easy enough, even at night, but the smaller details disappeared; I nearly rolled my ankle as I moved towards the tallest stone, near the centre of the circle. Stepping closer – more carefully this time – I held out both hands.

As before, I intended to hold my hands a short distance away. But as soon as I got near the stone's surface, it was as if it were a magnet pulling me in; I could not have avoided touching it if I'd wanted to. There was power here, of that there was no question: I felt its current surging through my veins. Closing my eyes, I started seeing shapes dancing against the black interior of my eyelids. At first it was the stones themselves, glowing yellow-green as if I were seeing them through night-vision goggles. Then the picture zoomed out, like a satellite image of cities by night, except that I knew somehow that these were not cities but other places like Callanish. Other sources of power.

I saw stars flashing by, rising and setting over the horizon, and faces I didn't recognize, flickering in and out of focus. It was overwhelming, and yet I could not pull my hands away – or would not; it was hard to tell the difference.

Eventually, the sensation ebbed away. I was once again capable of opening my eyes, of breaking contact with the stone. I let myself simply drop down onto the grass, heart still racing, senses still reaching out. I felt shell-shocked, and at the same time completely alive. Raising a trembling hand, palm to the ground, I stared at my fingers as I felt a tiny trickle of water running down from them.

The next thing I knew, I was being shaken awake. For a second I thought I must have dreamed it – but no, I was lying on the damp grass, the central stone looming large against the stars. Eric was standing over me, and the sky was no longer black, but royal blue: almost dawn.

"Are you alright? Don't sit up too quickly." He put his hands on the back of my skull, and I realized he was checking for bumps and bruises.

"I didn't fall," I said, surprised by how scratchy my voice sounded. "I was sitting down… I guess I just fell asleep. What time is it?"

"Not sure. Almost five, I think? When I didn't see you near the end of the night, I figured you'd gone back to the cottage; it only occurred to me later that you might come and do something like this. Come on, get up; it'll cause a commotion if somebody finds you still napping here once it gets light out." He helped me to my feet, which I appreciated; I had slept more deeply than could have been expected under the circumstances, but my body was registering the reality of having dozed off on rocky ground in the damp sea air.

As we walked back to the cottage, I couldn't help feeling as though I was slightly in disgrace. "Was I wrong to go there?" I finally asked, once we were inside.

Eric sighed. "Go take a hot shower and get changed, before you really get chilled through. Christ, I sound like my mother," he added under his breath. "Then we can talk."

I followed his suggestion, and found a pot of tea made when I emerged. "Not a risk-taker, my ass," he grumbled, motioning for me to sit down.

"What?" I asked, genuinely confused. "You said to come back later, when there weren't people around."

"I didn't mean no people around at all," he replied. "I meant curious onlookers, groundskeepers, that sort of thing. Not totally by yourself in the middle of the night. It's nothing to mess around with."

"I know that."

"No, you don't. You should have had someone there with you. You should have had…" He trailed off, shaking his head, although I couldn't help wondering if what he was really annoyed about was that I hadn't brought him, specifically, along.

"You know what? I think I do know. Do you want to know what happened when I touched that stone?" Hardly taking a breath, I launched into a detailed account of exactly what I had experienced; it was difficult to put into words, but was certainly fresh in my mind. "And then I had water running out of my fingertips," I concluded, sitting back slightly. "The next thing I knew, you were waking me up. But I didn't dream it."

"I don't think you dreamed it." He sat back as well, his eyes a little wider than they had been before. "But you know, you're lucky it went well. Usually it's best for new people to ease their way in – dip their toes in the pool gradually – and only tackle the big stuff with some guidance. Especially here, right now. This is an unusual place, even by our standards. You've basically just done the equivalent of going straight from the wading pool to the high diving board. Or, you know, casually walking up and picking up a live high voltage wire in your hand and wondering why people are worried."

Thinking of how it had felt to be connected with the stone, I could see his point. "So, you thought... what? That I'd gotten blasted away and hit my head or something?"

"Well, that sounds a little dramatic, but... yeah, pretty much. But you seem to be fine, so I'll get off my soapbox," he said, grudgingly. "How do you feel now?"

I had to think about it for a minute. "Tired," I replied, glancing out at the quickly brightening sky out the east window. "And stiff. But I feel... kind of invigorated, too."

"I bet. We're only a week out till the full moon; by that time it'll be so powerful that we can hardly get near that centre stone, let alone touch it. But tell me – has it changed anything?"

CHAPTER THIRTY-FIVE

The experience at the stone seemed like it should have changed everything, but I still had no answers.

The clock was ticking towards the lunar alignment that had drawn the magicians – and myself – to Callanish. I was partly impatient, and partly dreading it. Impatient, because particularly after my night at the stone circle, I couldn't wait to see what impact the rare full moon would have – on the stones, on the magicians, on myself. But it also felt like a giant wall across the calendar that I could not yet see past. Reading between the lines of my conversations with Eric, I had the distinct impression that they would be leaving very soon afterwards. And what I would do when that happened still remained to be seen. In my heart of hearts, I wanted to keep this strange fairy tale going, but I still could not imagine how to make that happen.

I started finding excuses to cut short the training sessions with Eric and Ben. Despite their generosity, and their apparent faith in me, I was still making no progress. Instead, I took to repeating my midnight visits to the standing stones: more cautiously, to be sure, but in the presence of that energy I found that I could make things happen. Small things, odd things, things I could not predict or control, but it was something.

As the days drew closer to the twenty-first, my solo practice sessions became harder to keep a secret. By the time the performances were winding down in the wee hours of the mornings, more and more of the magicians were coming up the road to bask in the growing power of the megaliths. I left the field earlier and earlier each night to try to give myself time, and slipped back down the slope when the hour grew late and I was no longer alone.

I had thought I was doing it all very quietly, but my disappearances had not gone unnoticed.

On the afternoon of the twentieth, I walked down to Flora's to meet Ben for my usual fruitless attempt at a magic lesson, but found Eric waiting for me at the gate, his posture stiff, his usual grin absent.

"What's wrong?"

He turned on me with a stare that almost made me back up a pace. "Why have you given up on us? You hardly even show up to the performances the last few nights. You've got a gift and we both know it, so why are you running away from it? If you want to go, just go. Pack up and run away to Canada, go back to whatever it is that you do."

For a moment, I just stood there with my mouth open. "I'm not running anywhere; I'm just trying to figure stuff out."

"Well, I hope you've figured something out, because we'll be gone the day after tomorrow." Turning on his heel, he stalked off, hands stuffed into his pockets, head down.

"Eric!" Whether my words were carried off on the wind or if he was just too angry to listen, he did not respond.

Cursing under my breath, I ran after him, calling his name again. I was catching up to him and he was continuing to walk away: definitely too angry to listen. "Just stop, alright?" I finally came up level with him and grabbed his arm. "Stop. Okay. Look.

I'm sorry. I should have said something. You've been far nicer to me than I had any reason to expect, and I shouldn't have just buggered off like that for the last few days. But I just... I needed some space to think. If there's anybody who knows how overwhelming all of this is, it should be you. No, just hear me out," I added, holding up a hand when he seemed about to interrupt. "I'm sorry I didn't tell you more. And I know this is the eleventh hour here, but you said yourself that you didn't make up your mind straight away when you first came. And before I make some kind of decision that's going to turn my life upside down, I need to know that I can handle it. Myself. I needed to see if I can figure out how to make this work on my own."

"Nobody does this entirely on their own," he said, some – but not quite all – of the heat gone from his voice. "Not even the likes of Raffaele or Sébastien, so don't think their DNA makes you an exception."

"I know. I know. And I'm not trying to say that I've got nothing to learn, or that I won't need help – a lot of it – if I do wind up staying. But after everything with Isabella, and the weirdness I feel now from some of the people here, I realized that if I'm going to do this, I'll have a hell of a lot to prove. And a long time before anyone judged me on my own merit. So I had to see if I could do it with just what I've got to work with."

"Do what, exactly?"

"Well, there is this." I took a deep breath. This would be my first real test. I lifted my hands, palms up to the grey sky, took another breath, let my eyes go slightly out of focus. Another breath, and a feather of doubt brushed across my mind: could I recreate any of this, away from the stones, with someone watching? But then, from my left hand, a jet of water erupted, cut an elegant arc through the air... and missed my right hand entirely, splashing down on the tarmac just past my boot. I looked from the splatter of water back to Eric's face. "The aim needs some work, obviously."

His expression changed completely, and I realized then that I hadn't been the only one with doubts about whether I could really learn to use magic. Somehow that made me like him more than blind faith would have. "That's amazing."

I shrugged, though my heart was racing. "Depends on your basis of comparison." By the standards of the people around me, it was kid stuff. Actually, I suspected that there were probably ten-year-olds who could do better. But it was something. "I needed to prove something to myself before I tackled anyone else. Even you."

"And so... does all this mean you do want to stay?"

"I think so. Yes. Yes, I do." There was a surge of adrenaline with this terrifying admission. "I do still need to go home, and settle some things up – pay some bills, pack some bags – but I want to come back to this. Just... not under anybody's wing. I'm happy to be your friend, and I know there are things that you, and Ben, and everybody else can teach me. But not as your protégé, or your pet project. I need to be able to do this standing on my own two feet."

Leaning in, he put an arm around my shoulders. "I'd expect nothing less. Just... don't disappear next time, alright?"

"So, what happens now?" I asked, as he stepped back.

"Well... The show packs up early tomorrow night. Earlier than usual, around eleven, so that we can all go up to the stones and watch the moon. And... okay, strictly speaking I'm not supposed to tell you this, but what happens there is only for insiders."

"Isn't it public property? Anyone can just walk in the gate."

He nodded. "There's... let's just say, you wouldn't see it all if you weren't invited."

"And I'm not invited?"

"It's not up to me. The thing is..." He made a hand gesture, clearly trying to figure out how to explain it. "If you really want to join us, if you're sure – it's not quite as simple as just saying 'okay, I'm coming along'. There's people to talk to, stuff to... You kind of have to get approved. Not that I think they'll say no," he added, as I opened my mouth to protest. "But just... there are a few people here whose opinions matter. With what you can do already, and who your family is, and the fact that you've got people like Ben on your side – trust me, I wouldn't be having this conversation with you right now if I thought there was any chance they'd say no. But it's something that has to happen."

"And if it doesn't happen right this minute, then what?"

He held out an open hand. "Then I do what Ben did for me. I find out where we'll be next, write it down for you, and hope to hell you show up."

I considered what he was saying. He wouldn't be telling me any of this if he didn't think I belonged. I wouldn't be having this conversation either, I realized, if I hadn't already made up my mind. The rest was all details.

"You might have to write it down for me anyways," I said. "Because I have a flight to catch on Monday - god only knows what I'm going to tell my family about what I'm doing – but you don't have to worry about me coming back."

"Good."

"But whatever it is that we – that I – need to do, to make this official... Is it something that can be done right now? Today? Because I've waited twenty-five years – hell, maybe my whole life – to be here right now, and I don't want to miss my chance to see what's going to happen tomorrow night."

Eric stood back another step, nodding, not saying anything. Then a smile spread across his face. "We haven't got much time. Let's go."

CHAPTER THIRTY-SIX

Eric led the way back down the road to Flora's house and rapped on the door. Colleen answered, her smile dropping several degrees when she saw who was there. "I'm sorry, Colleen," he said. "Is Ben in? I really need – Heather really needs to speak with him."

She disappeared, leaving us waiting on the doorstep, but a moment later Flora ushered us in to sit at the kitchen table, then left us alone when Ben emerged.

"What is it?" he said, his expression serious.

"Nothing bad," I replied immediately, my words tumbling out in a rush. "But I made up my mind; I mean, I'd like to join you – all of you – if you'll have me, but Eric says there's some formalities that need to be done, and I wanted to know if we can go ahead and do that today."

"Before you lose your nerve?"

"No – I mean, not really. It's not that. But I'd like to do it in time to see what happens at the stones tomorrow night."

"She's got it, Ben," Eric said. "She's got it nailed. She's taught herself."

Ben cuffed him – lightly – on the side of the head. "Heather's right beside you. 'She' is the cat's mother. What?"

He was looking at me, since I had let out a small nervous laugh. "Nothing. It's just that I haven't heard that saying much since I was a kid." Somehow it seemed like a good omen to hear one of Granny Chrissie's favourite maxims at this critical moment.

Ben rolled his eyes. "Well, at least you were taught some manners."

"Anyways," Eric interrupted, with emphasis. "I don't know if I remember everything I had to do when I joined. I don't know if I even knew everything that got done; did you have to do anything behind the scenes?"

The older man shook his head. "No. You're building this up in your memory into more than it was." Turning back to me, he continued. "Heather, the main thing you've got to do is see somebody we sometimes call the oracle. Her name's Sofia…"

"I met her," I said. "Very old lady who reads palms, right?"

Ben looked surprised. "That's the one. You'll have to go and see her – I can take you over, though I can't guarantee she'll see you during the day – and tell her what it is you're proposing to do. She'll take the measure of you, and speak with some of the other older folk. If all goes well, then she'll formally invite you to join us."

It sounded very much like a job interview to me, although I refrained from saying so. "I guess I've done all the preparation that I possibly can for this. Let's go and see if she'll give me the time of day."

Both of them came out with me, but Ben told Eric we would see him later. "There's no need to turn up with a crowd, and Sofia knows me."

"All right," Eric said, sounding reluctant, before giving me a reassuring pat on the shoulder. "Knock 'em dead."

I followed Ben along the upper road, to the last house before the small cemetery overlooking the loch; if he found the idea of an extremely elderly lady staying next door to a graveyard as morbid an idea as I did, he didn't say. Before we could mount the front steps, the door swung open and I saw Sofia herself standing there. In a housedress and a shawl, she would have looked like any other old woman but for the intensity of her eyes.

"Come in, Heather Ross," she said, as if Ben were not even there.

Entering the small house, I let her lead me into a tiny room draped with silks. The effect of stepping out of a typical Scottish front hall and into what looked for all the world like the interior of one of the magicians' tents was jarring, to say the least. I sat where I was told, and wondered who was to speak first.

Sofia settled that question for me. "You have learned a great deal since last we met. You stand on the precipice of a great decision: which way would you jump?"

"I want to come with you," I said, trying to sound confident. "I want to be a part of this world."

"Why?"

The most obvious question, and yet not exactly the one I had been expecting right off the bat. "I think…" Shaking my head slightly, I corrected myself. "Because I belong here. I am one of you."

"Because of your birthright."

"No." This time I shook my head for her benefit, not mine. "Because of who I am."

She did not argue the semantics. "Give me your hand, child."

I offered my left hand, all too aware that it was trembling. Sofia studied it for what felt like a long time, did the same with my right, and repeated the trick that made my veins glow silver – slightly less unsettling the second time, but only slightly. After that, she simply stared into my eyes for a minute or two, while I tried valiantly to hold her gaze. "It is enough," she said at last. "You may go."

Was that it? I stayed where I was sitting, unsure what to do. Clearly, I had been dismissed, but was she going to speak to the others? Had I passed muster so far? When it became obvious that no other answers were forthcoming, I stood up and sidled out of the house, feeling troubled and not a little annoyed.

Ben was leaning against the front gate, but stood up when I came out. "Don't worry, darling, Sofia's always a bit cryptic. It'll be fine."

"Did you have to do this?" I asked, as we turned back down the road.

"It wasn't Sofia, in my time – though it was by the time Eric came – but yes, I did. We all did, whether we're born into this or not. It's what you'd call a rite of passage, I suppose."

"And do they ever say no to anyone?"

He made a face. "By the time it gets to the point of someone coming to see the oracle? Not that I've seen. I'm sure it's possible – otherwise why would they do it? – but usually, if someone's at the point of asking for a judgment, it's because they know, and others do too, that they've got the gift."

I hoped he was right. "How will I know when they've decided?"

"You'll know."

CHAPTER THIRTY-SEVEN

When the knock came at my door just before six o'clock the next day, I ran to it, wondering if it would be a messenger. It was Eric. "Have you heard anything?"

He shook his head. "I still don't know. I'm sure they'll tell you soon. But it's the big night; do you want to walk down with me?"

"Isn't there anything you need to do? I don't want to be in your way."

"You won't. I'm all set."

The village was still quiet. I was one of the few outside the circle of the magicians who knew that this would be their last night here; the regular visitors would arrive at the usual time, and perhaps be disappointed when they closed up early.

Halfway there, I stopped him by the side of the road. "Eric, no matter what happens, this has been the most amazing three weeks of my life."

"It's going to be fine, Heather. You don't have to do this."

"Even if you're right," I countered – hoping that he was, "I still need to say it. I would have found my way here regardless – I had figured it out, and I guess somebody might still have worked out who I was – but this never would have been the same without you. I wouldn't have seen any of this in quite the same way. It's been a long time, actually, since I made any new friends, let alone a magician friend. And even if that's all I go away with, it's worth it."

"Thank you," he said, pulling me into a bear hug. "I haven't shown you quite the dashing love affair that your great-grandma had," he added, chuckling.

"I'll take friendship over a tragic romance any day."

Stepping back, he gave me a theatrical pout for a second. "Really?" Behind him, the carnival lights began to come on, indistinct though they were against the early-evening sky. "Nah, just kidding. Come on, let's go."

We walked the grounds, finding the food tent erected once more; I tried all the flavours of the Turkish Delight this time. Eric came with me into the menagerie, through Claire's tent and a few others, before finally saying that he needed to go and prepare his own performance. Just as the words were out of his mouth, though, we were interrupted by Luke, who came up panting as if he had run far and fast.

"The oracle…" he puffed. "Sofia…" Taking a huge gasp of air, he grinned at me. "You're in."

"What?" Eric and Ben had told me to expect it; I had not been able to come up with a good reason why they would not take me. But still, it came as a shock.

The second surprise was when Eric grabbed me up off my feet and whirled me around. "I knew it," he said as he set me back down, slightly dizzy but none the worse for wear. "Congratulations. I'll see you later – no vanishing act this time." With that, he was off.

Luke kissed me on the cheek. "Welcome to the club, cousin. You're in for a treat."

It was official: this was my last visit as a spectator. After Eric's performance, I wandered from one tent to the next, knowing that there was no way I could see them all this evening – but now I knew that I had time. I assumed would have to start at the bottom, probably in the ticket booth or something, but some day, there would be a tent on a field like this that belonged to me.

When the lights started to dim at ten-forty-five, there were many people checking watches and wearing expressions of disappointment or disbelief, but by a little after eleven, they had cleared out; the magicians began to file across the back-field shortcut in twos and threes, heading towards the standing stones. I waited for Eric and fell in with him and Claire, and we were barely halfway there when I noticed the full moon, hovering just above the ridge of hills in the distance. I thought I could feel the faint hum of the power source even from this far away.

"We'll get a better view from nearer the stones," Claire said. "I was just a little girl the last time; my parents didn't let me come close."

"Why is it so powerful?" I asked, as we resumed walking. "What is it about this phenomenon?"

They both gave me blank looks in the moonlight. "Honestly? I have no idea," Eric said. "I've tried coming here on my own, at other times, and the site always has something, but it's no comparison. But I don't know what it is about any of the places we go. I just know it works. Sorry to be disappointing," he added. "But I have no great mystical enlightenment."

I decided that there was time enough later to wonder about the why and how of it all; if this was a once-in-nineteen-years event, I had better get out of my own head and into the experience. When we got within sight of the stones, it was akin to walking into a wall of water; the energy coursed through and over me, humming in my ears and resonating in my chest. Just inside the central ring, some of the magicians – the older ones, it looked like – had formed a ring of their own, hand in hand at several paces out from the main stone.

"We'll have our turn," Eric said to both of us. "Don't worry. But first, we can watch the moon."

On a small rise of land just past the stones, a few dozen magicians were gathered, with rather the air of a community fireworks display: one family even had a blanket spread out on the grass for their two young children. Eric rather gallantly offered me his jacket to sit on, but I found a rock big enough for both of us. I had been coming here at night for several days now, but all my attention had been focused on the energy of the stone circle, and trying to work with it. I had not yet taken the time to truly look around, to see how the landscape was transformed at night. The moonlight cast a pale silvery glow over the scattered lochs and low mounds of heather, shining bright enough that I could see a faint shadow behind us. And as we watched, it seemed that the moon itself skipped across the southern horizon like a slow smooth stone, just kissing the peaks to the south.

I could have called it a worthwhile night for the sight of the moon alone, but eventually Eric rose from our rocky perch and called my attention back to the stones.

"What... is... that?" I asked, jaw hanging open. The elder magicians were still in their ring near the centre, but were now slowly moving round, still hand in hand, and chanting something formless and low. But that wasn't what had startled me. What was truly astonishing was that I could now not only feel the energy surrounding us, but I could see it as well. A pulsing beam of silver, not unlike a lightning bolt, was emanating out of the top of the central stone, and spreading into a canopy overhead; it was widening as we watched.

"It's time." He was grinning, but in a way that looked almost nervous; clearly the adrenaline rush was not exclusive to first-timers like me. Taking my hand, he led me to a spot just outside the ring of stones, where a larger circle of magicians was forming. Claire took my other hand, and soon we were joined all the way around. When the last link fell into place, a current ran round the circle and the silver light overhead expanded to cover us as well; beneath its shelter there was a veritable downpour of energy as we too began to move, in the opposite direction from the smaller circle. I felt as if it was soaking right through my skull, touching parts of my brain that had never before been used, and connecting me somehow to everyone there.

I should have been dazed, or astonished, or high on adrenaline, but what I felt instead was the most profound sense of calm and well-being; this had been missing my whole life and I had never known it was absent. I could watch my doubts disappearing, like embers rising away into the night: I was a magician now, and this was my place.

CHAPTER THIRTY-EIGHT

"Are you sure you need to go?" The tents were gone, the field cleared and looking as though it had never been subjected to the comings and goings of hundreds of people.

"Yeah, I do." I was standing outside Kestrel Cottage with my backpack at my feet. "I need to tie up some loose ends at home - make sure my house is looked after, pack a few things I want to have with me, have a visit with my mum and dad, that sort of thing." I would be partially honest, for now, I'd decided – tell my family I was taking a leave to do more travelling.

Eric ran a hand through his hair. He didn't have a bag over his shoulder, but it was clear that all the magicians were packing to leave town, one way or the other. "How long will you be?"

"Not long. I don't know – three weeks or so. Don't worry, I'll be back."

"You'd better be. And get a phone that works over here next time, so I can find you if you disappear again." He pulled something from his pocket: a card, and a pen. Turning me around by the shoulder, he used my back as a writing desk. "Three weeks, is it?" He wrote something else, then handed the card to me. "I'll hold you to that."

THE MAGICIANS' CARD

Still looking at him, I ran my thumb across the surface of the paper, knowing what it said even before I looked. It was the magicians' card.

A troupe of MAGICIANS from parts unknown – Nightly performances to astound and amaze!

I flipped it over. This time, there was a phone number – along with three words: *Hill of Tara*.

"It's in Ireland," he elaborated, then took my hand and kissed it. "Don't be late."

ABOUT THE AUTHOR

Lori Zuppinger is a historian by day and writer by night. She lives in Toronto with her husband, son, and a grouchy polydactyl cat. In her non-writing free time, she goes to a lot of concerts, plays a lot of board games, and wears a lot of knee socks.

Lori can be found at:
(Twitter) @ratherawkward
(Instagram) @escapistwriter

Stay tuned for more on the magicians!
The Magician's Walk is coming soon.

Made in the USA
Middletown, DE
05 July 2017